JENNY HAMBLY

DEDICATION

To mum and dad,
Thank you both for giving me my love of books!
(And mum for introducing me to Georgette Heyer.)

Thank you, Dave, for giving me time and putting up with a few
burnt dinners!

Thank you, Sean, for being an extra pair of eyes and a stalwart
supporter!

BACHELOR BRIDES BOOK 2

CHAPTER 1

The air in the drawing room at Danesbury Manor was so thick with tension it could have been cut as neatly as the slices of seed cake that lay untouched on the small table, next to the rather austere lady who was presently busy pouring out a cup of tea.

"So, your year of mourning is finally over, Sophie," she said, her voice as brittle as the delicate china cup she held.

Sophie winced at the wealth of insincerity and irony couched in that one word; mourning.

"Come, come, child," she continued impatiently. "You can hardly pretend that it was a love match! Your husband was old enough to have been your grandfather!"

"Great-grandfather more like!" sneered Alfred, seventh Earl of Lewisham, forgoing the tea and taking a deep gulp of claret instead. A thin, red rivulet snaked down his chin as he continued almost before he had swallowed. "Thought he'd keep me out of the succession by mounting a girl just out of the schoolroom! The miserable old goat! Cost him a pretty penny too. Would have been laughable if they hadn't been pennies that should rightfully have been mine!"

"Alfred!" his wife protested.

"Sorry, m'dear," he mumbled unconvincingly, taking another swig from his glass.

Sophie felt a bright red flush steal over her cheeks but clasped her hands tightly around her reticule, determined not to give him the pleasure of a response. They had taken an early dinner at only four o'clock, but the lack of any other company had unfortunately encouraged Lord Lewisham to join them almost immediately.

Rowena, Lady Lewisham, turned her pale, wintry gaze back towards her guest. "As I was saying, your year of mourning is now up. I cannot fault you for the quiet way you have spent it, although I own, I was surprised that you chose to stay at the Dower House rather than return home to your family. However, I should not think that you will bury yourself there for the foreseeable future? I cannot imagine what you can have been doing to amuse yourself."

Sophie took a delicate sip of tea whilst she formulated her response. 'You would know if you had ever condescended to pay me a visit,' did not seem wise. Edward had warned her to expect a cool reception from his heir and his wife. Even so, he had suggested she stay at the Dower House after his death and had provided her with an indigent distant relative, Agnes Trew, as a companion. *You must continue to develop your character and independence,* he had advised. *Go back to your family too soon, and you will be drowned in their endless needs and demands.* He would be turning in his grave at the behaviour of his nephew and his wife. Both the topic of their conversation and the style in which it was delivered, showed a lack of breeding and good manners he would have deplored.

Putting down her cup, Sophie gently stroked her reticule as if for reassurance. "Reading mostly." Ignoring the rude exclamatory noise that issued from Alfred, she continued. "But you are right. I think a change of scene would do me some good."

For the first time, Rowena's mouth approximated a smile, (if a somewhat sour one). "Ah, your mother will be pleased to have you home again."

Although she clearly could not wait to be rid of her, Sophie found it hard to take any real offence. Edward had been very keen to keep Alfred, (whom he described as a weak, snivelling, maw-worm with few morals and even less sense), out of his shoes. As two previous wives had failed miserably to furnish him with an heir before throwing off this mortal coil, he had decided on one last throw of the dice. Not wishing for the inconvenience, expense, or effort of going to town, Edward had looked about him. Sophie had been local, young, beautiful, and came from a large, impoverished family, (the last asset being of prime importance as it had made him eminently acceptable and he had taken it to be a promising indicator of her likely fertility). To close the deal, not only had he very generously provided for her family, but he had also agreed to leave Sophie the bulk of his unentailed fortune in the event of his death - if she had not conceived at that time. Only the knowledge that her deceased spouse would have thoroughly approved of her actions, gave her the courage to drop her next words into the conversation.

"I do not intend, at present, to go to my old home."

"Oh?" said Rowena, raising an enquiring eyebrow.

"No, I am thinking of going to town," Sophie said quietly.

The quality of the silence was now rather like the unnatural calm before a storm hits. Whilst Sophie had been living a quiet, frugal existence, Alfred had been able to keep his simmering resentment towards her under control, now that she was free to do as she pleased it was close to breaking point. His usually somewhat bovine gaze now resembled more that of an enraged bull.

"Town? Town?" he spluttered. "Can't wait to waste your blunt on fripperies, I dare say! Barely a year up and you are going off gallivanting, probably ready to catch some other poor unsuspecting fool in your toils, eh?"

"Alfred!" His good lady did not so much as glance in his direction, but her tone silenced him in an instant. "It is understandable that you should crave some amusement," she conceded. "Is your mother going to accompany you?"

Sophie could not fail to notice the exaggerated intonation Rowena placed on the word 'mother' or the frequency with which she used it. On the surface, her enquiries were innocuous enough, but anyone of any intelligence would have picked up the sneering conde-scension behind the words and the implication that she was not quite a respectable person.

"No, my husband's cousin, Lady Renfrew, has invited me up for a visit."

This time the stilted silence had a slightly stunned quality.

"Aunt Lavinia has invited you for a visit?" Alfred finally repeated slowly. "Ha! She'll eat you for breakfast!"

"Or treat you like an unpaid servant!" chimed in his wife. "I have to admit I am surprised, a high stickler, Lady Renfrew."

"Indeed, she is," Alfred agreed with some feeling. "I don't like you girl, won't pretend I do, but I wouldn't wish Aunt Lavinia on you." He had straightened his posture at her very mention. "Wouldn't stay with her if I were you. If you must go, take your mother and stay in a hotel."

Rowena gave Sophie a hard, shrewd look. "Of course," she said slowly, "everything hinges on your ambitions. If you are on the catch for another husband, Lady Renfrew will certainly be able to introduce you to the most exclusive circles."

"I do not wish for the most exclusive circles or another husband." Out of the corner of her eye, she saw Alfred slump back in his chair at her words. "However, Edward encouraged me to continue with my studies of the classical world, and I can think of no better way to do it than by travelling."

"Continue your studies?" repeated Alfred, clearly flabbergasted. "Uncle Edward married a bluestocking?"

"Well, you can view those broken bits of stone Lord Elgin dragged back from Greece," Rowena said doubtfully. "Although why anyone would want to, is beyond me. I believe they are on show at The British Museum."

Sophie knew that it would probably be better to keep the reach of her plans to herself for now. She and Miss Trew had kept themselves occupied over the last year by planning a fantastical trip, a sort of grand tour. However, neither of them had ever really expected to put that plan into action. It was only when she had received the most unexpected invitation to visit with her husband's cousin in town, the notion that she could use her time there to acquire the various permissions and letters of introduction she would need to travel across Europe had begun to take hold.

"Yes, I will visit The British Museum, of course, but I was thinking of travelling on the continent to see such wonders in their natural context. I have a desire to stand in the places where momentous events have happened," she asserted boldly, feeling that somehow saying the words aloud would make her plan feel real.

Alfred had begun to turn an interesting shade of purple. "Have a desire to ...momentous things..." he spluttered. "A girl as green as you and a widow, travelling alone? The only momentous event likely to happen is that you will drag this name even further into the mire than you did when your grasping little hands persuaded you to bed a man who was on the verge of senility. You will end up a whore to some dispossessed poet or foreign gentleman..."

"Enough!" Rowena snapped.

Sophie was on her feet, ready to flee. She had never enjoyed brangling.

"Wait." Rowena rose and looked imperiously at her visitor. "Although I cannot condone the extreme frankness with which my husband has spoken, I must agree with his sentiments, however inelegantly expressed. You have very little experience of the world at large, and so are hardly equipped to look after yourself on such a journey. Go to London, but postpone the rest of your plans, at least until you have formed some acquaintance with whom you could travel."

Sophie had an inkling that there was more than a grain of common sense in this advice, but she was too inflamed by Alfred's grubby insinuations to back down.

"Thank you for your advice," she said stiffly. "But I will not be alone; Miss Trew will accompany me."

Sophie marched back towards the dower house with a vigorous energy not usually associated with young ladies of quality, alternately grumbling under her breath and re-reading the letter from Lady Renfrew that had been a secret source of hidden support throughout the visit. How glad she was to be leaving this place! The only thing she would miss was the library, a room in which she and Edward had spent many happy hours. She suspected it would now be largely left to gather dust. She slowed as she neared her destination and briefly closed her eyes, her mother's strident tones ringing out across the small garden in front of the house announcing her presence.

Sending a swift prayer of thanks that she had already accepted the invitation, and so could not easily be persuaded to change her mind, she stuffed it back into her reticule. Letting herself quietly in, she cast a wistful glance at the staircase, but before she could set foot on it her mother's piercing voice carried clearly to her ears.

"It seems to me, Miss Trew, that you cannot be a fit

person to look after my poor, widowed child. When I think of the heartache and worry I have suffered, that she should be alone at such a time with only a stranger to bear her company. My dear, sweet girl."

Dear, sweet girl? This, from the woman who had never missed an opportunity to criticise her, and had accused her of being a changeling on more than one occasion? Feeling it would be unfair to leave Agnes alone with her any longer, she squared her slender shoulders and reminded herself that she was no longer a schoolroom miss to be bullied or used as the repository for all her mother's countless disappointments. She was that rare thing: an independent widow of means.

Pasting on a smile that was as false as her mother's sentiment, she pushed open the door.

"Mama, what a surprise. I am sorry I wasn't here to welcome you."

That lady's already ample bosom, swelled with indignation, putting the seams of the wide-striped calico dress she wore under severe pressure. Narrow, close-set eyes swept Sophie from head to foot, making her conscious of her muddied boots and wind-swept russet hair.

"So, this is what happens when you are left to your own devices! You look quite wild! Am I a visitor of so little importance, then, that you do not feel it necessary to run upstairs and change your boots, remove your bonnet, or drag a brush through your hair?"

Sophie eyed her mother's heightened colour warily, she was clearly agitated, and experience warned her that only careful handling would prevent one of her spasms coming on.

"Mama, I didn't want to keep you waiting any longer than necessary," she explained, calmly removing the offending bonnet. "But, of course, I will run upstairs and tidy myself up."

As she reached the door, Sophie cast an apologetic glance at Miss Trew, who was sitting ramrod straight on the edge of her chair. At least her mother could find nothing to fault in her appearance – she was as neat as wax, her mousy-coloured hair pinned in a rigid bun from which not a single tendril dared escape.

"Wait!"

Used to her mother's capricious ways, she came back into the room and sat down, folding her hands neatly in her lap.

"How you did *not* expect a visit from me after that letter you sent me, I do not know! What is this about you going to stay with Lady Renfrew? If she is that condescending woman whom I met after the funeral, I cannot think what you mean by it. She looked at me as if I was something that had crawled out from under a stone!"

"If that is true, I am sorry to hear it," Sophie said. "She was very formal when I met her, but polite. The invitation came out of the blue and I think it very kind of her to think of me."

"Kind? If that woman proves to have a kind bone in her body, I will own myself amazed!"

Feeling that anything she might say would only inflame her temper further, Sophie remained silent.

"What about your family, Sophie? Alcasta and I would be only too happy to accompany you to town. Whilst you were in mourning, you could be of no use to us, but now you are in a position to hire a house for us all. Perhaps this Lady Renfrew could introduce us to some people? Just in a quiet way, you know. Alcasta must make her come-out next season or she will be quite on the shelf, some experience first would be most helpful."

Go back to your family too soon, and you will be drowned in their endless needs and demands.

Sophie knew a cowardly impulse to withhold her full intentions until she was far away but conquered it. Raising her large, green eyes from the floor, she plunged in. "Before I can help any of my sisters, I need some experience of the world myself, Mama. It was Edward's wish. I intend to visit London only for a short while and then travel on the continent as far as Italy. I want to see for myself the remains of antiquity. I would love to go as far as Greece, but it is too dangerous at present as the Ottomans and Greeks are fighting over Athens..."

"You always were a selfish, unnatural girl," her mother interrupted. "Perpetually having your head in a book rather than trying to attract a potential husband or help in any useful way! Have you any idea how difficult it is to bring up – never mind out – five girls on a shoestring? No, of course you have not, and why would you care? You have not changed; you are still obstinate and ungrateful. What useful experience will you get to help your sisters, by looking at a lot of old stones or paintings that I'll lay odds are indecent, is beyond my comprehension!"

Suddenly clutching at her heart, she sank back onto the sofa. Miss Trew was on her feet in an instant with the smelling salts she seemed to think necessary that every lady should keep close to hand. Kneeling in front of the afflicted lady, she waved them under her nose.

Sophie, more used to her mother's theatrics, stood her ground. Emotional blackmail, she knew, was an open book to her. She did not miss the moment her mother surreptitiously half-opened one eye to monitor the effects of her half-swoon.

"I did my duty when I married," she stated calmly. "Edward and I did not keep secrets; I know to the last sovereign how much you benefited from my marriage, and I am happy that it was so."

She meant it. Even though her family had been willing to sell her to a man who, as Alfred had so scathingly pointed out, had been old enough to be her grandfather, she harboured no resentment. She was not of a romantic disposition and had understood it was a business transaction that benefited all parties, securing her future and removing her from an uncomfortable position in her own family's household. Her mother's only words of wisdom at the time had been to assure her that her husband was unlikely to live for many more years, especially if she did her duty by him. Sophie had failed to appreciate this advice either then, or now.

Unexpectedly, she and Edward had developed a companionable affection for each other. He was surprised and pleased to discover that behind the beautiful façade, lay a brain and an insatiable thirst for knowledge; she to realise she was to be not only allowed unlimited access to his impressive library but that he was happy to guide and teach her.

"Oh, get off me, woman!" her mother suddenly snapped, pushing Miss Trew away and making a miraculous recovery. "Your father would rather spend his blunt on his pack of dogs or his fine horses than his family, as well you know!" she complained bitterly. "But as it is useless to argue with you, I will only say this – don't come running to us when you have committed every folly going and find yourself shunned and without a character!"

She carried on raining criticism on her daughter's head all the way to her carriage. When Sophie returned to the drawing room, she found Miss Trew still perched on the edge of her chair, pale and silent. Kneeling in front of her, she took both of her hands in her own.

"Don't set any store by it, Aggie," she said. "It is all drama, mother lives for it."

"Did you mean it?" Miss Trew asked, raising her slightly myopic gentle, grey eyes. "Are you really intending to put our plans into action?"

Sophie squeezed her motionless hands. "I know, Aggie. It is a daunting thought, is it not? However, we are two intelligent, reasonable women. Is the continent such a wild place that two modestly behaved ladies cannot quietly make their way across it without being kidnapped by a wicked count or falling into a swoon at the sight of a naked statue? Did we both not thoroughly enjoy Marianna Starke's book, *Travels on the Continent*? We planned to use it as our guide, remember?"

Miss Trew nodded her assent. "It is true that remarkable lady has made the journey more than once," she conceded. "But Sophie, I am a vicar's daughter, until I came here to live with you, I had hardly been more than a few miles from my village.

London will be a great adventure for both of us, and I am looking forward to it. Do you not think you might perhaps meet some like-minded acquaintances there with whom you could travel onwards?"

Although Sophie had found it easy to ignore Rowena, Miss Trew's echoing of her sentiments was harder to dismiss.

She laid her cheek in her friend and companion's lap. "I suppose I might be getting a little ahead of myself," she conceded, striving to hide her disappointment. "How about we give London a try and then see how we feel?"

As Agnes gently stroked the disordered locks in her lap, a stray beam of sunshine suddenly set their red and gold tints alight.

"When you get to London, I predict you will be gay to dissipation and quite happy to bask in the glory of all the admiration you will attract," she said softly. "Now, upstairs with you. It will take your maid a good half an hour to brush the tangles out of your hair!"

CHAPTER 2

S ir Philip Bray, ex-captain of the 15th Hussars, pulled up his smart curricle outside his town-house in Brook Street, jumped down with a liveliness that belied the fact that he had been on the road for two days and nodded for his groom, Vaughen, to carry on to the stables in the mews behind. Having spent a very pleasant few days with his friends, the Athertons, celebrating their son's christening, it might have been expected that he would be happy and relaxed. However, he took the steps up to his front door two at a time, with a restless energy that suggested otherwise.

"Pleased to have you back, sir," said his butler, accepting the impressive many-caped greatcoat and hat offered to him.

"Thank you, Stanton," he replied with his usual charming smile.

"You will find quite a pile of correspondence on your desk, sir," he said apologetically and then paused as if uncertain of quite how, or if, he should continue.

Sir Philip was surprised; it was not like Stanton to be cagey or indecisive.

"Was there something else?" he asked quietly.

"Nothing important, sir, just something a trifle irregular," he admitted.

"Go on," Sir Philip encouraged him gently.

Stanton cleared his throat. "Ah, one of the letters awaiting you was hand delivered, sir."

Sir Philip merely quirked an eyebrow.

"By a lady," Stanton finished.

"Ah, I see. Thank you, Stanton," he murmured before striding off towards the library.

Throwing himself rather carelessly into the chair behind his desk, he swung one booted leg over the arm and frowned at the large pile of missives before him. When that didn't make them disappear, he thrust out his large, but perfectly manicured hand, and scooped them up. Most of them were clearly invitations to the latest round of dinners, balls, card or garden parties or heaven forbid, musical recitals, on offer.

He hastily discarded all of them without compunction. It only raised false hopes in the breasts of all the matchmaking mamas who were, he knew, speculating on when he would finally settle down and set up his nursery. Why turning thirty was seen to be such a watershed event was beyond him, but everyone seemed to think that he would now settle down and do what they saw as the responsible or respectable thing. Even though he had just witnessed a splendid example of married bliss, he believed George and Rosalind Atherton were the exception rather than the rule, and he felt no great desire to emulate them.

That left him with three items. The first was tied

with a pink ribbon and smelled of his latest widow's perfume. He tapped it against the desk twice and then threw it on the discard pile too. He was very much afraid the lady in question was about to suffer the same fate. He had always made it clear that he was not on offer for the long-game and favoured discretion in all their dealings, it seemed she was trying to redraw the lines of engagement, but calling in person at his house was a step too far.

The next letter had his instant attention. Swinging his leg down to the floor, he leaned forwards and leant both arms on the desk, looking down at it for a long moment. The paper was crumpled and dog-eared, but he immediately recognised the rather loopy scrawl. Harry Treleven. A crooked smile twisted his lips, and he slowly relaxed back in his chair as the image of his old friend and lieutenant swam before him. Tall, with broad shoulders tapering to a narrow waist, golden hair, sapphire-blue eyes flashing with mischief and excitement, his nose aristocratic, his bearing proud – Harry had owned a dash and gallantry that were irresistible. He had not known what fear was. A superb and reckless horseman, he had risked his neck on the most dangerous brutes. He had also excelled in swordsmanship and had proved to be a first-rate shot.

He had never been the same after Waterloo. The light had gone out of those eyes, he had taken to drink, and the mischief he had gotten into had been of the more serious kind, culminating in a duel. It had been unfortunate and avoidable as the lady in question had enjoyed a string of affaires, but Harry had broken the unspoken gentlemanly code: whilst in his cups, he had been indiscreet. The much put-upon husband, Lord

Worthington, had only two choices; call him out or become a laughing stock.

As one of his oldest friends, Sir Philip had, of course, been his second. Although exasperated that his friend was behaving so recklessly, he had not been unduly concerned. Everyone had known Harry was the better shot by far, including his opponent, but they also knew he didn't have a mean bone in his body. It was expected he would delope and indeed, that had been his intention. It was not until he had begun raising his arm, that Sir Philip had noticed how much his friend's hand was shaking; he had been dipping deep again – in itself not an unusual occurrence – however, the night before a duel it was ridiculously careless, even for him. The pistol had gone off early, severely injuring his opponent. It was extremely doubtful he would last the night and it had been up to Sir Philip to get Harry safely out of the country.

"Don't worry, old chap," he had laughed, embracing his friend before stepping onto the smuggler's vessel destined to take him across the channel. "As there is no peace to be found on the land, I will become a pirate and live by the sea!"

That had been five long years ago, and he had not heard from him since. Nor had anyone else. The irony was, the cuckold had survived his ordeal, after all.

Sir Philip blinked, and a small glass filled with a deep red liquid swam into view. Stanton must have placed it there whilst he had been wool-gathering. One of the side-benefits of ending the war with France was having access to a good wine from Bordeaux. He fortified himself with a sip before opening Harry's letter.

Hello, old chap,

I hope you are thriving in the land of our birth. I expect you have a wife and a bevy of children by now.

After spending the last few years at sea, I have put my privateering days, and many questionable deeds behind me and have landed in Pisa. My eyes have been opened! Tower, dome, arch, and spire are my new horizon. Everywhere is colour and light, and even the voices that speak a language I don't understand, are music to my ears.

It is ironic that I find that damned poet, Byron, here. I, who have lived the life of a Corsair, end up in the same city as the charlatan who writes about one! His latest mistress, the Countess Teresa Guiccioli has recently arrived, so perhaps the many fair ladies of this city, who are generous and friendly to a fault, will be safe from his philandering ways.

I have been fortunate enough to be befriended by one of these good ladies, as I am plagued by a recurring fever which has left me low. Maria Trecoli is an angel beyond compare; without her unremitting care, I would probably have departed this life.

I would dearly love to shake your hand again, my friend, there is something that I need to share with you. I would risk all and travel to you if I could, but in my current state of health, it is impossible. If you are passing this way, you can find me near the quay, in lodgings at Parte di Mezzogiorno. Just ask for Maria, and you will find me.

Your friend, Harry Treleven

P.S. Perhaps you could let my mother know I am alive.

Sir Philip sat ruminating over this missive for some time before turning to his last communication.

In sharp contrast to Harry's well-travelled document, this one was pristine, folded with precision, and had just one, neatly printed word adorning the cover. Philip. The crisp, neat strokes commandeered his attention as effectively as its author's voice always had. As usual, it was short and to the point.

Philip,

I expect you are back by now and trust you will call on me at your earliest convenience.

LR

Would he? He frowned down at the summons. It was certainly not convenient; the urge to make all haste to Italy was strong upon him. However, his lips curled into an affectionate smile. He would, of course. He owed his godmother too much to deny her anything. After his mother had died attempting to provide him with a sibling, who had been stillborn, he had frequently divided his summers as a child between his godmother, the Athertons and the Trelevens.

It was the usual custom to receive guests in the drawing room, but he was not at all surprised when he was shown to the library. Lady Renfrew thrived on being unusual. The more masculine surroundings of this room exactly suited her no-nonsense demeanour, as well as being the cosiest in her large townhouse.

She sat by the fire, a small glass of claret on a table beside her, along with a book, and a rather splendid gold and blue enamelled snuffbox. She wore a long-sleeved high gown of dark ruby levantine and a quite exotic gold turban upon her steel grey locks. She was still a very handsome woman with a pair of piercing silver eyes. Even though he towered over her, she nevertheless managed somehow to look at him down her long, straight nose.

"So, you finally managed to fit me into your hectic schedule," she drawled, her voice unexpectedly low for a female. "I suppose I should be grateful."

A smile of genuine amusement lit his deep, blue eyes as he crossed the room in three quick strides. He took her surprisingly delicate hand in his, swiftly dropping a kiss on it before glancing surreptitiously around the room.

"Ah, don't tell me. You have finally run out of suitors and so pine for the company of a mere godson! Or is that fat, old cockerel I found strutting around you last time, hiding behind the curtain?"

Lady Renfrew gave a low, deep chuckle. "You leave poor Percy alone. He has been my friend since before you were born!"

"He has been deeply in love with you since before I was born," he grinned. "I can't decide if he has nerves of steel or none at all!"

"Hrmph! Enough of your insolence, you are a good for nothing here-and-therian with more money than sense! It is time and more you settled down. But no, you are one of those who prefers to chase women rather than catch 'em! As for your latest, a prime article if ever I saw one!"

A slightly pained look crossed Sir Philip's face. "I suppose it is too much to hope that you will develop some subtlety in your dotage," he parried.

Lady Renfrew gave another rich, throaty laugh. "Beyond praying for! I give the word with no bark on it, as you well know. But you're right, it is none of my business and not what I asked you to visit me for."

"Asked?" he said gently.

"Oh, sit, you're giving me a crick in the neck!"

Taking the chair on the other side of the fire, he accepted the glass of claret his godmother's butler unobtrusively offered him, crossed one leg over the other and unconsciously started drumming his fingers against the armrest. None of his barely suppressed impatience passed by the eagle-eyed lady opposite.

"Open your budget!" she said. "What tom-foolery are you about to embark upon?"

As she had invited Harry to stay many times during his childhood, he had no compunction in revealing his latest news.

When he had finished, she gave him a long, considering stare. "There is, of course, no question, you must go to him and bring him home if you can. His poor mother has never been the same since he left."

"I know. I will visit her before I leave. It is the least I can do."

"Still blaming yourself, then?" his godmother sighed. "I won't waste my breath trying to persuade you otherwise, but you will have to wait a couple of days to visit Lady Treleven, she is out of town but is due back by the end of the week."

Sir Philip nodded, not at all surprised that she seemed aware of Lady Treleven's movements; little went on in town without her somehow knowing of it.

"I have a couple of things I need to tidy up first, anyway," he said briskly, getting to his feet and bowing politely. "Oh, what was it you wanted of me, Aunt Lavinia?"

"Oh, only to give you your birthday present," she said nonchalantly, reaching for the beautiful snuffbox beside her.

"Thank you, it is..." he suddenly stopped. He had thought how lovely it was when he had given it a cursory glance earlier. It was gold, inlaid with beautiful blue panels, but as he flicked it open with a practised flick of his left hand, he discovered that instead of snuff inside, there was a small, miniature portrait. He carefully took it out and raised his quizzing glass to his eye. It was perfectly executed. Raven black hair curled attractively around the face of a young woman, and it seemed her blue eyes stared rather wistfully up at him. He could almost have been looking at a female version of himself.

"Mother," he said softly, his lips curling into a small smile. Finally, he raised his eyes and looked across at the woman who had stood in her place throughout his formative years.

"Thank you, I only have one portrait of her alone."

"Don't get all sentimental on me," Lady Renfrew said briskly, clearing her throat. "There is one, small thing you can do for me, Philip."

"Name it," he smiled.

"Amelia Feversham is giving a ball on Thursday night, I would like you to escort me to it."

The smile slipped. Lady Feversham had two unmarried daughters: Lucinda, who was painfully shy in his presence – making it nearly impossible to hold a conversation – and Harriet, who was quite the opposite, making it almost impossible for him to edge a word in. However, in this instance he could hardly accuse his godmother of matchmaking as it was no secret that there was no love lost between them.

"There's no need for you to look blue-devilled! Amelia Feversham has hardly two sensible thoughts to rub together, and those that she does have are inane or gossip-filled. Her mother was just the same! She also has an inflated sense of her own importance, always has had! To be truthful, it pains me to gratify her by making an appearance at her ball, but I have a guest coming to stay for a few days who will need entertaining. She is my cousin's widow, and as Percy is off to Newmarket for the racing, I thought you might escort us. However, if it is too much trouble..."

Bending over her hand again, he kissed it and then her cheek. "It will be my pleasure, Aunt Lavinia, but if your cousin is anything like you, God help me!"

Not more than half-an-hour later, Lady Lewisham and Miss Trew were shown into the library.

Sophie had felt a growing amazement and excitement within her as they had made their steady progress through town and she had experienced a snippet of the constant life and noise that filled the metropolis through the window of her carriage.

However, she had also felt increasingly nervous as they approached Berkeley Square; if she had been shown into a formal drawing room and been received with due pomp and ceremony she would have felt out of her depth. Instead, she felt the tension at the back of her neck ease, and her shoulders relax as she took in all the cosy informality of the library. Her memory of Lady Renfrew had been somewhat fuzzy, but the animadversions on her character made by Alfred, Rowena, and her mother had left her expecting the worst sort of tyrant. Only the thought that Edward had been outwardly crusty but quite likeable underneath had given her the courage to proceed with her plans. However, she had the advantage of catching that redoubtable lady off-guard, and one glance at the slightly rumpled, sleepy figure by the fire with a book open on her lap, melted her fears.

"Lady Renfrew," she said, stepping quickly into the room and offering a quick, graceful curtsey. "Please, do not get up, you look so comfortable there. The library has always been my favourite room in the house too, how wonderful that we share a love of books."

In other circumstances, Lady Renfrew, who was indeed known as a high stickler, might have given such informality and familiarity of address a deserved set-down. But in this case, she did indeed find herself at a disadvantage; the joint effects of the claret and the warm fire had lulled her to sleep and so she was not at her most needle-witted. Besides, it was a hard heart indeed that could remain unmoved by the warmth and vitality encapsulated in Sophie's genuine, wide smile. It transformed her already pretty face into an animatedly beautiful one. Her colouring; rich auburn hair, jade green eyes, and creamy skin were not quite in the usual style either.

"You'll do," she murmured obliquely.

CHAPTER 3

Sophie and Lady Renfrew developed an almost immediate affection for each other, perhaps more deeply felt because it was such a rare occurrence for both of them. The former because her experience had been largely confined to her own household and Lady Renfrew because she did not suffer fools gladly and found the world unfortunately populated with a great many of them. Like her deceased cousin, she found it refreshing to be in the company of a young, unaffected lady with a lively, enquiring mind. Even so, after one stimulating discussion ranging from the merits of poets as diverse as Blake and Byron, she gave Sophie a word of warning.

"Although I enjoy our talks, my dear, it would not be wise to show yourself too clever in general conversation. Tonight will be your first real introduction to society, and it would be fatal to your reception if you are seen as a bluestocking."

Sophie felt herself bristling. "As I have no great

wish to figure in society, the thought does not worry me over-much," she shrugged.

She immediately realised her mistake as she found herself on the receiving end of what some disgruntled unfortunates who had experienced it before her, had named Lady Renfrew's basilisk stare (although never to her face).

"Don't be a fool, girl!" she snapped. "What is the use of all the intelligence in the world if you have no common sense or think that book-learning can replace experience or sound advice? You know nothing of the society of which you speak! Think of Byron, whatever your personal opinion of him, the fact remains that he was courted by everyone a handful of years ago when he first published 'Childe Harold's Pilgrimage'. Foolish women even carried his miniature around to swoon over if they could not get an introduction! A few years later, he had to flee abroad or be ostracised from the very society who had put him on a pedestal. Do you really wish to follow his example? If you must go abroad, go because you want to, not because there is no better alternative."

Until that moment, Sophie had not realised how much she had enjoyed the easy affection which had developed between them. An awkward, antisocial child, she had found it difficult to develop close relationships with her mother or her sisters, with whom she had little in common. On the outside she had had all the advantages; her appearance and figure were pleasing, her aptitude for learning, drawing and the pianoforte were exceptional, but she had always preferred to lose herself in a book than join in with the constant quarrels and arguments of her sisters. She had often slunk away to hide in a quiet corner of the library. Her father had not minded and had even gone as far as inviting her to hide in his study once or twice – perhaps not wisely telling her that he could not blame her for seeking a retreat from all the infernal squawking that always seemed to be going on as he often did so himself.

Mistaking her quietness for meekness, her mother had thrust her into social situations she had no desire to be in and discovered the underlying streak of stubbornness that lay within. From the start, she had refused to play the game of flirtation with her would-be admirers; not because she was contrary, but because she genuinely did not enjoy it. She found she had little in common with any of them and did not find their flow of empty nothings interesting or flattering. Her husband had been the first person, apart from her governess and perhaps her father, to find no fault with her character, and his cousin, Lady Renfrew – an original herself – had also seemed to accept her for who she was. Casting herself on her knees at Lady Renfrew's feet, she took her hand in both of her own.

"I am sorry," she said, blinking rapidly to hold back the sudden, unexpected tears that threatened. "You are right, of course. I would be foolish to ignore your advice. It is just that I have never felt quite comfortable at balls and dinners where I am expected to converse without actually saying anything."

Despite her annoyance, Lady Renfrew's lips quirked into a sympathetic smile. "Well, it is a skill you must learn, my dear. Unless you are royalty or an eccentric old lady like myself, you have very little choice!"

"Are you not finished yet?" said Sophie rather plaintively to her maid, Burrows.

That lady gave a heartfelt sigh and said in a nononsense tone, "If you would stop fidgeting as if you were sitting on hot coals, my lady, I might be able to tame these unruly tresses of yours! His late lordship, God bless his soul, hired me to make sure you always looked your best and he would turn in his grave if I let you go out looking anything less than perfect!"

Knowing this to be true, Sophie submitted but her eyes watered as yet another section of her locks was pulled and pinned quite ruthlessly.

"You'll do," Burrows finally said.

"You look beautiful," breathed Miss Trew.

Sophie had never really given too much thought to her appearance, but perhaps surprisingly, her bookish husband had. He liked beautiful things and had taken an unexpected delight in seeing her becomingly turned out and had even sent for a seamstress to take her measurements and provided her with a quite extensive wardrobe. She had always happily donned whatever Burrows had laid out without ever really paying any great notice to her attire. However, a year of mourning had given her a new appreciation for her raiment, and as she gazed at her reflection, she smiled as she took in the details of her dress. Both striking and elegant without being ostentatious in any way, it was at heart a simple white round dress, composed of tulle over a white satin slip; it was the trimming of tulle, chenille, and pearls at the bottom of the skirt, arranged in wreaths of corn, flowers, and roses that set it above the ordinary.

Her hair was dressed artlessly, falling in ringlets to either side of her face and adorned only by a simple spray of pearls, the motif repeated in the pearl necklace that graced her long, slender neck.

"I wish you were coming, Aggie," she said, turning towards her as Burrows briskly rolled on her white kid gloves.

"I would not know how to go on at such a grand affair," she replied, handing Sophie her wrap and delicate ivory fan. "And anyway, you have no need of me with Lady Renfrew to chaperone you. I shall be quite happy at home with a book. Now down with you, quickly, if I am not much mistaken, I heard a carriage arrive a few moments ago."

Sir Philip had excused himself from attending dinner, feeling that he was doing more than his duty in escorting his godmother and her relation to the ball. When Sophie entered the room, he had his back to the door.

"Ah, there you are, at last, child," Lady Renfrew said, pushing herself to her feet.

Sir Philip executed a neat turn at this form of address.

"Sophie, Lady Lewisham, my cousin's widow, let me present Sir Philip Bray, my godson."

It was not often words failed Sir Philip or that his famed charm and address deserted him, but the vision standing in front of him was so far removed from the image he had formed in his mind of an older lady, not unlike his godmother, that he was left speechless for a few moments. His eyes were not so incapacitated, they swept comprehensively over the young lady before him, taking in the elegance of her figure and dress, the way the simplicity of the white brought out the rich red tones in her hair and the arresting green of her eyes.

He belatedly offered a rather stiff bow, only his innate good manners preventing him from displaying the annoyance he felt that his godmother should have played him so. If she thought for one moment, that a beautiful widow would distract him from his present purpose, she was much mistaken.

Sophie's curtsy was also rather mechanical. She had not given their escort much consideration at all, but her first impression was that his eyes almost precisely matched the blue of his elegant, swallow-tailed coat. An inane thought that irritated her and that irritation only grew when she felt his assessing glance rake her from head to toe. Sophie did not have a very high opinion of extremely handsome men. She had met a few at the local assemblies and been forced to conclude that they were often brainless and almost wholly concerned with their appearance and conse-quence. They were free enough with their compli-ments, but she felt sure it was only because it reflected well on themselves both to say them and to be seen with someone who deserved them. Unfortunately, and to the despair of her mother, she had not developed the habit of being irresistibly pleased with a young man merely because he possessed the happy art of making her pleased with herself.

It was not a promising start to their evening, but despite his annoyance at being so clearly manipulated by Lady Renfrew, it did not take the astute Sir Philip long to realise that Lady Lewisham had had nothing to do with it. He did not think vanity was one of his failings, but it was, he had to admit, an unusual occurrence for the young, beautiful ladies of his acquaintance to observe him with an expression of some disdain, rather than throwing him an arch look or one of maidenly confusion. Either way, as he did not intend to devote his evening to any beautiful young ladies, it was neither here nor there.

Once he had seen his godmother comfortably situated, he disappeared in the direction of the card room, a show of uncharacteristic rudeness which did nothing to improve Sophie's initial impression of him. If Lady Renfrew was disappointed that Sir Philip had disappeared, she did not show it and pausing only to introduce Sophie to an eligible partner, quickly settled down with her cronies.

Sophie had thought she knew what to expect from a ball, but she very quickly realised that what passed for a ball at a local assembly in the country, was a far cry from a London affair. Lady Feversham's ballroom was of a far grander scale, and she had certainly not spared any expense. Once she felt confident with the steps of the first country dance, Sophie marvelled at the number of beeswax candles that glittered everywhere. She estimated there must be at least three hundred of them. They were reflected in the many gilt-edged mirrors that adorned the walls as were the many coloured satins and silks of the ladies and the shimmering jewels that graced their arms, necks, and hair. The hum of voices greeting one another, the tinkle of laughter, added to the strong scent of the many flowers that festooned the room, made Sophie's senses swim for a moment. She was quite glad when the dance came to an end and she could partake of a refreshing draught of lemonade.

She had hardly recovered when Lady Feversham descended on her. A very attentive hostess, she insisted on introducing Sophie to a succession of eligible dance partners. Sophie found herself thankful for the first time that her mother had insisted on arranging impromptu dancing sessions for both her daughters and their friends and ensured that Sophie had attended the local assemblies. Both the country dances and the quadrille proved to be lively and surprisingly enjoyable. The novelty of dancing with strangers, the snatches of new conversation and the exertion were exhilarating. So, when Sir Philip made an impromptu check on his godmother, he found Sophie all sparkling eyes, heaving bosom, and rosy-cheeked and impulsively solicited her hand for the next dance, just as the waltz struck up.

Sophie found herself in a dilemma – she could hardly decline without appearing unacceptably rude after having danced all evening – nor did she wish to upset Lady Renfrew, yet she felt strangely reluctant to experience her first public waltz with this man. It was not just his rude appraisal when he had first met her, or the fact that he was their supposed escort and had not been near them all evening that made her hesitate; she found something undefinable about him, unsettling. As it was, Lady Renfrew decided for her.

"That's the ticket," she boomed, "you won't find a better dancer, Sophie, so off you go."

As soon as Sir Philip's arm encircled her waist, Sophie's mouth went dry. As the music started and he swept her across the floor, their eyes locked and Sophie gave herself up to the rhythm of the dance. For quite some time, neither said a word. The other dancers became a blur to her as he led her effortlessly around the room with only the lightest of touches.

"You dance very well, Lady Lewisham," he finally said with a rueful smile.

It transformed his countenance from forbidding to charming in an instant.

"You must have been married very young," he said softly.

His words broke the spell that had bound her, which was a relief for she had been feeling strangely breathless and unlike herself.

"I was just turned nineteen when I was married, not a particularly young age at all. If you mean that I was young to be married to my husband, Lady Renfrew's cousin, I cannot disagree."

"And were you happy?" he murmured into her ear. Somehow the question felt like a caress.

Sophie nearly missed her step, surprised at such a personal enquiry. "I find your question an impertinence on such a slight acquaintance," she protested. "My happiness then or now, is none of your concern."

Fortunately, at that moment, the dance came to an end. Sir Philip bowed and returned her to Lady Renfrew. Feeling a little out of sorts, Sophie swallowed a groan as Lady Feversham appeared in front of them. This time, however, her attention was directed at Sir Philip. She had a young lady in tow. The likeness between them was remarkable, each had a long nose and a receding chin, and bright, darting eyes.

"Ah, Sir Philip, there you are. So naughty of you to

wait so long to dance when there are so many young ladies desirous of a partner," she smiled indulgently, tapping him on the arm with her fan. "How fortunate for you that Harriet has a dance still free."

Sir Philip said all that was polite and dutifully rejoined the throng of dancers.

Sophie found herself unaccountably warm and light-headed and so made her way towards the end of the room which was less crowded. Her eye was caught by a very young lady, who stood on the edge of a group of giggling girls who were surrounded by a crowd of attentive young gentlemen. She was very pretty, with bright blonde hair and limpid blue eyes, but looked uncomfortable, her face a little pale and her eyes searching the crowd as if looking for someone. They met her own briefly before moving past her. Sophie was just considering introducing herself when a very modish lady in a beautiful rose satin gown glided past her with a light step, her hands held out towards the shy wallflower. Sophie saw a small smile of relief curve the young lady's rosebud mouth and satisfied that she had been rescued from whatever awkward situation she had found herself in, sat on a sofa that was mostly hidden by an impressive fern, displayed in a large urn.

"They say he was quite *ancient* and has left her a *fortune*."

Sophie had relaxed back into her chair and had been cooling herself with her fan, but this overheard snippet had her full attention. Snapping it abruptly shut, she peeped between the fronds of the plant. She could just make out the rather buxom form of a lady in a rather low-cut ruby coloured dress, she half turned to her companion, revealing a countenance that would have been pretty if not for the rather petulant droop about her full lips. A gold ornament glittered in dark hair that was piled unusually high. "It is fitting is it not, that such a blatant gold-digger, should be courted by all the fortune-hunters. The tables are turned, and if she is not very careful, she will find herself caught in her own trap!" the unknown lady tittered.

The titter was returned, and Sophie saw the gloved hand of her companion wave the pretty fan she had been languidly wafting herself with, at her friend.

"It is true that at least three of her partners are known to need a rich wife, but you surely cannot include Sir Philip, he is very well-off and seemed very taken with his partner, I thought."

They carried on their slow progress around the room and Sophie lost sight of them. Feeling somewhat deflated and even more overheated than before, she stood up quickly and stepped back around the plant and into a room that suddenly swam before her eyes. She felt her arm taken in a cool grip.

"You are not well, Lady Lewisham, here, come this way," said a gentle female voice. "You are quite safe, I am Lady Isabella Hayward. I know just what will make you feel better."

A few moments later, Sophie found herself on a cool terrace and her vision cleared. She looked into a pair of understanding, intelligent grey eyes. It was the same good lady who had gone to the rescue of the wallflower.

"Thank you, I feared for a moment that I was going to faint."

"Yes, it is insufferably hot inside and such a sad crush, it is hardly surprising."

"I saw you earlier," said Sophie. "Approaching a young, pretty girl who looked a little distressed."

Lady Hayward nodded. "Yes, that was Miss Treleven. A lovely, young widgeon and hopelessly shy. She has been living quite secluded and to be thrown into a situation such as this is torture to her. I merely returned her to her mama but not before I had noticed you dive behind the fern! I am incurably nosy, you see, and had already determined that I would make your acquaintance!"

Sophie smiled, finding her honesty refreshing. "I am glad of it," she said. "I know so few people and have also been living quite retired from society."

"Of course, as a widow, that is to be expected. But I think you had been enjoying your evening until perhaps you overheard Lady Skeffington gossiping, as I think you were meant to."

"Like I was meant to?" Sophie echoed, bewildered.

Her new friend nodded. "You are a beautiful, young widow who is rumoured to be very well provided for. You are bound to be an object of gossip and conjecture at first you know."

Sophie let that sink in for a moment. "But why would Lady Skeffington want me to overhear?" she asked.

"Well, do not misunderstand me, Sir Philip is a very good, very old friend of mine and I love him dearly, but he is quite determined to remain single. I had hoped that he might follow my brother's example now that he has finally settled down, but sadly this does not seem to be his intention."

Sophie blinked, she had not thought herself in the least stupid, but she was finding this conversation quite challenging to follow.

"Are you saying that Lady Skeffington wants to marry him?"

The fair-haired lady before her laughed, revealing two very appealing dimples. "Oh, I am sure she does! She is also a widow, Lady Lewisham, who is not getting any younger and I do not believe her jointure is overly generous." She paused for a moment as if weighing her words. "Oh, you have been married, and though it is not good-natured or quite the thing to gossip, she started it, so I will tell you. She has made the stupid mistake of thinking a taste of her very obvious charms might do the trick, where all the hordes of innocent debutantes that have thrown themselves at him, have failed!"

Sophie's mouth dropped open at such frank talk. "She is his mistress?"

Lady Hayward shook her head, her golden curls bouncing around her animated face. Leaning a little closer, she murmured, "*Was* his mistress. He has been nowhere near her tonight."

"But what has all this got to do with me? I have never set eyes on him before today."

Lady Hayward's head tilted to one side as she considered Sophie seriously for a moment. "Lady Lewisham, you appear out of the blue, just after he has terminated their arrangement. You are younger than she is, prettier than she is, and he chose to ignore all the ladies in the room until he singled you out for the waltz."

"Ah, I see," she sighed. "And were all my other partners fortune-hunters?"

Lady Hayward linked her arm again with Sophie's and smiled. "No serious fortune-hunters have been invited. However, it is true that one or two of your partners need to marry money if they are prudent. But if they were charming and agreeable, what is it to you? If a woman has beauty, she may marry money; if she has money, she does not need beauty. You appear to have both, and so you have the world at your feet! Enjoy it! Only do not be surprised if you become the target of enmity from some who are not so fortunate and of a jealous disposition."

Sophie found herself smiling back, Lady Hayward possessed a joie de vivre, that was infectious. "Well, as I am not looking for a husband and will not be in town much longer," she said, her mind made up, "you are quite right, it matters not a jot. It does not reflect well on Lady Feversham, however, for she introduced them to me as desirable partners!"

Lady Hayward nodded in agreement. "But she has two daughters of marriageable age and Sir Philip, although not a marquis or an earl, comes from an old, respectable family and is very wealthy, as well as being extremely charming and well-looking."

"Surely, money cannot be of paramount impor-tance to her? When I think of what the candles alone must have cost tonight, never mind the refreshments!"

"I can see you have a lot still to learn about the ways of the *ton*, Lady Lewisham. It is a shame you are leaving town so soon because I think we are destined to be great friends and I would be happy to teach you. Suffice it to say, all is often not what it seems. I have a feeling you might be a case in point, now come, tell me all about your plans, for I can sniff out an adventure a mile off."

They returned to the ballroom together and slowly made their way towards Lady Renfrew, their heads close in conversation. Lady Hayward had just extracted a promise that Sophie would write to her about her adventures when they reached her.

"Ah, I wondered where you had got to," she grumbled. "Been making friends, I see. Well, Belle used to be a sad romp, but I am glad to say she has improved greatly since she married Hayward."

Instead of taking umbrage, Lady Hayward gave a tinkling laugh and leant down to kiss Lady Renfrew's cheek.

As she straightened, Sophie saw Lady Feversham wending her way towards them with another dashing young man in tow. She glanced over at Lady Hayward with a raised eyebrow. "Is he one?" she enquired with a slight smile.

"Yes," Lady Hayward confirmed seriously. "But very charming!" she added, sending them both into peals of laughter.

Sir Philip duly presented himself at the establishment of Lady Treleven. It was the second interview he had undertaken this week, and he expected it to be as unpleasant as the first. Lady Skeffington had at first shed despairing crocodile tears all over him and when he remained unmoved, taken to casting hysterical aspersions on his character, manhood, and mankind in general. None of which he had felt he particularly deserved, but he had cared too little to put forward any arguments to the contrary.

Lady Treleven had had some harsh words for him in the aftermath of Harry's duel. '*So, this is how you repay a friendship of longstanding and all the hospitality you have received in my household. I have treated you almost as a second son. I survived the fight against Napoleon, only because I knew you would look after Harry as well as anyone could in such a situation. No words could describe my joy when he arrived home, alive and with all his limbs intact. Yet not only did you not manage to keep him safe, but you also helped him in his foolhardy duel and then sent him packing abroad for no good reason as it turns out! If you want to be welcome here again, find him!*'

Each word had been a dart to his heart, for every one had only echoed those he had, for the most part, already said to himself. Lady Treleven had been reclusive for some years after Harry's disappearance, and it was only for her daughter's sake that she had now made a return to society, and as he avoided most social functions these days, it was years since their paths had crossed.

Acting on impulse, Sir Philip had not informed her of his intended arrival or the reason for it and so half expected her to refuse him entrance. However, to his surprise, he was given immediate admittance, the butler not even pretending to see if she was 'at home', and was shown not into the drawing room, but escorted directly to Lady Treleven's private sitting room, where she joined him not many moments later.

She had always been a beautiful woman – Harry's extraordinary good looks had come from her – and she was still very handsome, her bone structure would always ensure this was so, but her looks had faded, almost as if someone had gone lightly over her edges with an eraser. He was grieved to see the lines of worry and sadness which had etched themselves into her face. All this registered in barely a moment, and then, to his great surprise, he found himself caught up in a fierce hug that nearly un-manned him.

"Philip, you have come at last!" she said as she released him, only to take both his hands in her own. "Let me look at you!"

The astute blue eyes looked at him closely. "Still so handsome," she murmured, "but not as carefree as you used to be."

"Lady Treleven," he began but was immediately cut off.

"Oh, shhh, I was for too many years, Aunt Dorothea, to you, to become Lady Treleven when we are private."

He would have spoken again, but she stopped his words, putting her gloved finger to his lips. "Philip, dear Philip. I must speak before I can allow you to. Come, sit with me."

She led him to a sofa by the fire and sat next to him, still holding his hands, hers lost within his. Her eyes filled with unshed tears, giving them the shimmering brilliance he remembered and reminding him painfully of her son.

"I saw you at Lady Feversham's ball, but poor Henrietta had the headache, and I had to take her home before I could speak with you. I was hoping you would come and informed Stanley to admit you if ever you did. Philip, I am so dreadfully sorry," she paused

41

to dash away the drops that had now spilled over onto her cheeks.

He pulled her to him, enveloping her in a bear hug from which she emerged presently with a watery chuckle. "Enough, for I fear I have ruined your beautiful coat!"

Sir Philip returned her smile with complete unconcern. "I believe I have another."

Again, she took his hands. "Philip, I am finding it hard to put into words the feelings that are in my heart, so I will simply say this, I did not mean what I said to you in the deep agonies of worry I was suffering at losing my only son in such a way. You were not to blame, no one was, and I have missed you, my second son. At first, I thought that if I could not have Harry, I wanted no one, but that was all grief and foolishness. Please, tell me you forgive me."

Sir Philip kissed first one hand and then the other of the lovely woman in front of him, feeling the deep darkness that had long dwelled within him, lighten a shade.

"There is nothing to forgive. I too am sorry," he said. "I should not have stayed away. I took your words quite literally, you see."

Lady Treleven, raised her hands to cup his face. "Poor, foolish, Philip."

She watched, as a slow, wide grin transformed the sombre countenance before her. "I have found Harry," he said softly. "Or rather, he has found me!"

Lady Treleven closed her eyes. Silent tears trickled again from beneath her lashes. Sir Philip wiped them away with his own handkerchief.

"He is alive, then," she finally breathed.

He silently pressed Harry's letter into her hands, and when she had read it through several times, the narrow shoulders beneath her shawl began to shake, this time with laughter.

Sir Philip could not recall any amusing anecdotes in the missive and for a moment, was worried hysteria was setting in. The upset of seeing him and the shock of his news must have been too much. He was considering ringing for a servant when she raised eyes brimfull of amusement. "Do not look so worried, Pip, I do not need hartshorn! It is just so like Harry, to add as an afterthought the '*P.S. Perhaps you could let my mother know I am alive,*' bit. Now I know he cannot be at death's door!"

Her first instinct was, of course, to fly to him, but she was too sensible a woman, not to realise that she would only slow Sir Philip down and ruin her daughter's chance of a successful season.

She smiled confidently at him. "You will bring him home, I know."

She also insisted on giving him a large purse of money for the woman who had nursed him. "I do not know what manner of woman this Maria Trecoli may be," she said, "and I care even less. Make sure she wants for nothing!"

CHAPTER 4

When Miss Trew saw how set Sophie was on carrying out the trip they had planned, she buried her doubts and agreed to accompany her. Their visit to The British Museum to see Elgin's marbles had made quite an impression on them. The spectacle of headless and sometimes limbless statues – which nevertheless still held an echo of the grace and beauty of their original execution and in their natural setting within the Parthenon would have served the atmosphere of decaying grandeur well – in their present situation seemed only to highlight the fact that they had been ripped from their true home. They found they had some sympathy with Byron's view that 'Dull is the eye that will not weep to see, Thy walls defac'd...By British hands'.

The visit helped define the final itinerary for their journey. At first, daunted by the vast array of sights recorded in Marianna Starke's book and how long it would take to do even a quarter of them justice, they now agreed that they would make haste through France, before enjoying the experience of the Alps and then focus their experience on Pisa, Florence, and Rome. Miss Starke assured them that Pisa had not only been founded by Romans, but still held some excellent examples of classical antiquity as well as being the place where the revival of the style in the twelfth and thirteenth centuries could be seen. She maintained that 'Those persons...who contemplate the productions of the Greco-Pisano school as the earliest efforts of the reviving arts, cannot fail to be highly gratified...'

There was one other important visit that Sophie chose to make, but this time alone. It was to the offices of a Mr Pickett. He was the attorney Edward had entrusted with his business. She was conscious of the vague feeling of anxiety that always assailed her when she expected an extremely formal encounter. She was shown into a meticulously ordered office and greeted by a white-haired old gentleman in a black suit, his wrinkled face a testimony to his age, but his hazel eyes were astute, alive with intelligence, and held a lurking twinkle.

"Lady Lewisham, I am honoured to meet you," he said, bowing as far as his back would allow.

Sophie smiled. Somehow, he had put her immediately at her ease.

"I must offer my sincere condolences on the loss of your esteemed husband. Lord Lewisham was a remarkable man."

"Indeed, he was," she concurred.

"I must also congratulate you on attaining your age of majority," he said. "You are a fortunate young lady. The private fortune Lord Lewisham's uncle bequeathed to him is now yours to do with as you will. I am more than happy to continue to manage it for you, but if you feel you would prefer a younger man to take on the office, I can proffer some recommendations that might suit."

"Oh no," Sophie said. "That is not the purpose of my visit, I assure you."

She proceeded to explain her current plans. When she had finished the twinkle was even more pronounced.

"I see," he said. "You are an intrepid young lady, and I am happy to help in any way. I will acquire the passports you need, sufficient funds for your adventure and arrange for the purchase of a carriage in France. You will be much more comfortable with your own carriage."

"Yes, I think so too," she agreed.

"However," he added. "As you do not take a relative as your escort, would you mind if I offered you a few words of advice?"

"Not at all," she replied, pleased to hear an objective voice of reason. "I would be most grateful to hear them."

"Take a male servant, as well as your coachman, and make sure you impose your presence on any foreign innkeepers or officials. If you do not, you will find yourself a target for impertinence or fraud, at the very least."

Sophie thought about that for a moment and then nodded decisively. "I find your advice sensible, sir."

Mr Pickett looked pleased. He hesitated over his next words, however. "Please do not take offence, Lady Lewisham, but would you object if I offered you some advice of a more personal nature?"

She looked intrigued. "Not at all, although I cannot imagine what it might be."

He gave her a rather old-fashioned look and said in a tone more fatherly than official, "You are very young and very beautiful. I say that as an impassive observer, you understand. However, it would not be surprising if you came to the attention of some, shall we say, more worldly gentlemen?"

Sophie nodded, raising an enquiring brow.

"Well, I do not wish to cast doubt upon your judgement, my lady, but if you feel inclined towards such a one to the extent that you might consider the sacrament of marriage again, might I suggest that you consult me first, on the matter of settlements. You have a very healthy fortune, and I would like to see you well protected in such a circumstance."

"I do not intend to marry again," Sophie smiled. "But if such a thing were to occur, you may be certain that I will follow your advice."

Expecting Lady Renfrew to try to delay her departure, Sophie was both relieved and surprised when on the contrary, she proved most helpful, giving her letters of introduction to families she knew to be in Pisa and Rome, and assisting her in acquiring a male servant, a Mr James Squires, to help and protect them on their journey. She had found him through a charity she patronised that helped find employment for impoverished ex-soldiers. Tall and skinny, with a jaunty grin and a slightly devil-may-care attitude, Sophie was not convinced about him. However, Miss Trew reminded her gently that often all someone who had been down on their luck needed was a chance to prove themselves.

"You'll have to train him up," Lady Renfrew warned her. "I am ashamed to say that whilst we were happy enough to pack off raw recruits to throw in Napoleon's path, we were not so good at ensuring their continued well-being if they were among the lucky ones who made it home alive. Remember, not all scars are visible, but treat him with a firm but fair hand and I am sure he will be of service to you."

Sophie took her by surprise by hugging her fiercely as she departed. "I wish you could come with us, dear Lady Renfrew, I can never thank you enough for your hospitality and kindness," she said tearfully.

Unused to, and usually disapproving of such open displays of affection, that redoubtable lady nevertheless briefly returned the embrace.

"Ten years ago, I might have come," she said briskly. "But these old bones will no longer stand the nonsense. You can thank me by returning safely and coming for a proper stay. When you have got the travelling bug out of your bonnet, we will see about getting you properly established!"

Sophie had been looking forward to her first sea-crossing, but unfortunately, it did not meet her expectations. The weather had been inclement, and within an hour of leaving port the ship had been rolling in a most alarming manner, which had given her vertigo, followed by horrendous sea-sickness. It was a fortunate circumstance that Miss Trew had been unaffected and able to look after her with the assistance of her maid. She had been extremely grateful when she had stepped again onto dry land, and even then, the rolling sensation and feeling of nausea had taken some time to pass.

Their way through France proved largely unproblematic; travel was again a popular past-time and everywhere was set up well to accommodate the traveller. They found the roads were largely good, and if the signs of the revolution marred the beauty and edifices of several towns, the countryside as they approached ever nearer the Alps was clothed in vineyards and had a most pleasing aspect.

It was nearing dusk as they approached Dijon and they were fascinated to see a large party of women, colourfully dressed, down by the river, chatting and laughing as they washed an assortment of garments. As suggested in their guide, they found the Hotel de Parc a comfortable establishment with a good table and excellent wine. After a satisfying night's repose, they awoke early, keen to begin their approach to the Jura Mountains. They were thwarted, however, by Squires; the availability of cheap spirits at some of the establishments they had visited, had encouraged him to over-indulge and he had subsequently delayed them on more than one occasion.

Their coachman sat quietly, his face wooden – he did not approve of Squires and tried to have as little as possible to do with him.

"You leave him to me," said Burrows grimly. "I will fetch the useless good-for-nothing wastrel myself. I promise you he will soon regret the necessity!"

As she marched off purposefully towards the

stables, Sophie and Miss Trew exchanged an exasperated glance, which turned to one of sternly repressed amusement as Burrows re-appeared, pulling Squires along by his ear, his posture stooped and water dripping from his hair and face.

"A bucket of water soon put him to rights," she said with some satisfaction. "That'll teach him to go on the cut!"

Miss Trew, although not conversant with that particular term, got the general gist and decided to offer a little further encouragement in her own style, giving him a gentle but stern sermon on the evils of strong drink.

"I am sure you wish to be useful, Squires, but you would do well to observe what it says in Corinthians: 'Nor thieves, nor covetous, nor drunkards, nor revilers, nor extortioners, shall inherit the kingdom of God'. Peter also advised: 'Be sober, be vigilant; because your adversary the devil, as a roaring lion, walketh about, seeking whom he may devour.' You must mend your ways, or you will be lost."

Squires's head had begun to droop – although whether from shame or a thunderous headache was not clear.

"You will most certainly be lost," confirmed Sophie, her tone acerbic. "For unless you can give me your word that you will mend your ways and tread a more sober path, I will leave you where you stand!"

That got his attention. His head snapped upwards, his eyes widening with sudden fear. "Please, no mi'lady, do not leave me in this godforsaken land, miles from home and with nothing but the shirt on my back! I will leave off the strong stuff, I give you my word!"

"See that you do," Sophie said sternly before turning to her carriage.

Nothing that had gone before prepared them for the breathtaking, natural beauty of the Jura. As wild and sublime as promised, at times towering perpendicular cliffs hemmed them in, the claustrophobic feeling exacerbated as they passed under deep archways hewn out of the granite rock-face. This was often followed by the sudden, unexpected appearance of lush pastures or proud glades of beech or fir trees, climbing the valleys like silent sentinels to the passes beyond. Their first view of Lake Geneva and the impressive glaciers which enclosed it took their breath away, the natural magnificence and beauty that surrounded them more than compensating for any fatigue felt in achieving the prospect.

"You cannot now wish that you had not set out on this expedition!" Sophie cried, turning to her companion. "One cannot help but reflect on the insignificance of mankind when confronted with such a truly ancient and immovable landscape."

Miss Trew answered with a smile and her usual placid common sense. "The world God has created is indeed a marvel, and I must feel privileged to see first-hand some of his most sublime work. But even though we may seem insignificant, like ants crawling over a huge mound, it is the mind and labour of man that has carved these pathways through seemingly impossible terrain. God instructed us to 'be fruitful and multiply, and replenish the earth, and subdue it,' but I can quite see, that it would be a feat not to be desired or contemplated, that man would or could subdue such a place as this!"

The further they went into the Alps, the more the landscape defied their imaginations. Napoleon's excellent military road allowed for good progress, and the often winding terrain, bound by rock on one side and steep precipices on the other, frequently left them unprepared for the hidden treasures just around the corner. The pass over the Simplon was rich with imagery. A lush natural valley of rolling orchards and meadows emblazoned with flowers would be swiftly superseded by swollen waterfalls that if caught by the sun, could be turned into shifting rainbows of colour and light. At other times, peaks would be obscured by shifting cloud and mist that would lift just long enough to give a tantalising glimpse of isolated monasteries or ruined castles perched on remote outcrops, recalling to mind The Mysteries of Udolpho. At these moments, Sophie admitted to herself that although she had always disagreed with her siblings and berated Ann Radcliffe's novel as not worthy of any consideration, she could now appreciate how such a landscape could inspire such a fertile inner imagination.

Slowly, as they climbed ever higher, the temperate weather changed. Trees no longer flourished, and those that survived were bent like old men against the bitter blasts of cold wind that blew down from the icy peaks of the mountains. Some had been uprooted and thrown one upon the other, stopping just short of a yawning abyss, reminding them that their safe passage relied upon the mercy of natural elements outside of their control. The temperature continued to plummet as they approached an impressive glacier grotto carved from the ice. As they emerged on the other side, icy sleet started to fall, and they occasionally had to stop for the coachman and Squires, to clear away drifting piles of snow.

Sophie shivered and thrust her hands deeper into her muff. She was glad when they began their descent. Beneath them, a huge reservoir of water stared blindly upwards with its milky eye at the snow-filled clouds gathering above. She was heartily relieved when they reached the inn, ironically called Le Soleil, in the small hamlet of Simplon. The threatening weather had encouraged many other travellers to break their journey here, and they were lucky to engage the last remaining room. Sophie and Miss Trew would have to share the bed, with Sophie's maid on a truckle bed, jammed in one corner. However, it was clean and comfortable enough.

Unfortunately, there were no private parlours to be had, and the dining room was full to bursting with guests eager for their meal when they came down for dinner. Two long trestle tables ran almost the length of the establishment, but there was not enough space, even for two slender ladies, to squeeze themselves in. The noise, heat, and smell, from so many crammed together like cattle in a stall, was for a moment over-whelming, but the growl of Sophie's stomach outweighed such trivial disadvantages.

The proprietor, a small man with a fat stomach and an avaricious gleam in his eyes, obviously felt that no extraordinary civility was necessary when his coffers were so full. He eventually waddled his way towards them, waving one impatient hand before him as if to swat away flies. "Later, you will have to come back later."

Miss Trew immediately stepped back as if to withdraw, but Sophie grasped her arm in a tight hold. Although she did not like wrangling, neither did she like to be dismissed in such an off-hand manner. If the innkeeper had apologised and shown some regret for their inconvenience, she would have been happy to comply, as it was, his attitude, coupled with another timely reminder from her stomach that it was many hours since she had eaten, put paid to any such compliant behaviour.

Her time with Lady Renfrew had not been wasted, with a fair imitation of her basilisk stare, she looked the offending gentleman up and down as if he was something nasty that she had found on the bottom of her slipper. "It does not suit me to come back later," she said, icily. "You will find us a place, now."

"But Madame..." he began to protest.

"Lady Lewisham," she corrected haughtily.

Sophie was pleased to see the look of uncertainty that crossed his face. If he had thought that two ladies travelling alone would be easy to fob off, he was fast learning his mistake.

He stretched out his arms in entreaty, his tone slightly more placatory as he pleaded, "But what would Madame have me do?"

Sophie nodded to a dim corner; now the serving girl had moved, she could see a small, empty table.

"That will do."

The man before her looked even more uncomfortable. "But that is already reserved..."

"Perhaps, I could be of some assistance," came a calm, cool voice from behind her left shoulder.

A voice she had only heard during the course of one evening but which she recognised immediately.

Whirling around, she gazed at the gentleman in some astonishment.

"Sir Philip, whatever are you doing here?" she burst out.

His correct bow reminded her of her manners and colouring, she dropped a swift curtsy.

Ignoring her question for the moment, he turned back to the innkeeper. "I believe I reserved a small table?"

Sophie grimaced, why had she not thought of that?

The innkeeper was all obsequious smiles now and bowed so low he almost wiped his nose on his knee.

"As you say, sir, please, come this way."

"One moment, I believe there will be room enough for these two ladies to join me."

"But of course, it is the perfect solution," he smiled relieved, weaving his way across the crowded room with surprising agility for one so large.

Sophie turned to Miss Trew who was looking at her in some amazement. "Oh, do not look at me like that, Agnes. It is the outside of enough that we are treated with such insufferable rudeness, merely because a man does not accompany us."

"And that is an excuse for you also to be rude?" she chided gently. "Now, I suggest we accept Sir Philip's very generous offer or retire to our chamber."

Feeling like a gauche schoolroom miss, Sophie nodded and joined him where he stood politely waiting for them.

"Sir Philip Bray, this is my companion, Miss Trew," she said, aiming for a polite but business-like manner.

His bow was deeper than was strictly necessary for

a companion and the smile that accompanied it was friendly and open.

"It is a pleasure to make your acquaintance, ma'am," he said.

It was perhaps not surprising that Miss Trew was a little flustered at such attention and consideration from such a handsome and commanding person, but Sophie was surprised to see something suspiciously like a blush creep over her cheeks.

"And it is a pleasure to meet you again, Lady Lewisham, although quite unexpected. My godmother did not mention your intended journey to me."

"Nor yours to me," Sophie countered.

"And you are travelling alone?" he prompted.

"As you see," she replied, a slight challenge in her direct gaze.

"How very..." he paused as if searching for the right word, "intrepid."

It was perhaps fortunate that the soup arrived at that moment, for Sophie thought he might as well have said foolish and felt her hackles rise. She declined the offer of cutlery from the waiter as they had followed the advice in their guide and brought their own.

Sir Philip looked amused but said nothing, turning his attention to Miss Trew. When it was discovered that her father's parish was known to Sir Philip, they enjoyed quite a comfortable cose, and it was not long before he had, with considerable adroitness, drawn out of her all the information Sophie would have been reluctant to give about their plans.

Initially annoyed, Sophie found herself relaxing as he showed no inclination to criticise them but on the contrary, was all politeness and interest.

"So, how have you found your first experience of the mountain passes, Lady Lewisham?" he suddenly asked her, drawing her back into the conversation.

Happy to converse on such a general topic she replied with real enthusiasm. "Words cannot fully express how the magnificent scenes I have witnessed have impressed themselves upon my imagination! I had looked forward to expanding my mind and understanding upon this journey, but I had not before realised how such a varied and sublime natural landscape could speak to something within me that goes beyond the life of the mind, that touches something almost spiritual," she suddenly laughed. "I fear I am expressing myself poorly."

Sir Philip's lips twisted into a crooked smile. "On the contrary, your eyes express your feelings as clearly as your words." For a moment they had locked with his, burning like a green flame with an intensity that had scorched him.

"It is all God's creation, after all," Miss Trew commented quietly. "But I must say it has been a delight and an education not to know what might be waiting on the other side of every hill."

Sir Philip was silent for a moment as if lost in thought. "Wellington would not agree with you ma'am," he said eventually. "The secret of his success throughout the wars was knowing exactly what lay on the other side of the hill!"

"Ah, a soldier. I thought as much," Miss Trew said. "You were in the Peninsula?"

The trout they were served was delicious, and they spent an enjoyable meal discussing the differences between the mountains in Portugal and The Alps. Sir

Philip was happy to draw a general picture for them of conditions there but seemed reluctant to offer any personal anecdotes or expand on the reason for his journey, other than to say he had urgent business with an old friend.

He insisted on escorting them both to their chamber after dinner and even went as far as offering to act as escort for them as they made their descent into Italy. An offer which took all parties by surprise.

"You are all kindness," replied Sophie, all frigid formality again at the implied suggestion that they needed the mantle of a man to protect them. "But you are in a hurry, and we have managed very well so far. As I believe we will continue to do so, I will politely decline your very generous offer."

There was nothing for Sir Philip to do but bow and wish them goodnight.

"You do not think that it might have been a good idea to accept Sir Philip's offer, my dear?" Miss Trew asked when they were cosily tucked up in bed. "He would easily iron out any difficulties we might encounter, as he did tonight, and he is a charming companion."

Sophie turned to her, a mischievous smile lighting her countenance. "Oh, Aggie, I do believe you might be just a little bit in love with him!"

Miss Trew did not take offence, but admitted, "I should think every lady must fall a little bit in love with him, his countenance is so handsome, and he is so, so big! One cannot help but feel safe with him."

Sophie could hardly deny him his appearance, however, could not agree with the final sentiment. He had occasionally looked at her in a way that made her insides flutter, and it was not a sensation which she had enjoyed. If anything, he made her uneasy. It was then she remembered the bitter tones of Lady Skeffington at the ball.

"Tell that to his latest mistress, a widow he has discarded as he would an old coat!"

Miss Trew looked shocked, and Sophie felt a stab of remorse at destroying her rose-tinted image of him. "I am sorry, Aggie, but it is true. In accepting his offer of protection, I would perhaps save myself from the frying pan only to jump into the fire!"

If he were honest, Sir Philip was a little relieved that his offer had been declined. He was a man who generally kept firm control of his actions, with a clear head and an objective eye. These traits had saved his life and those of others, on more than one occasion. It was also true of his dealings with women. A very energetic man, it could not be expected that he would live like a monk, although his inherent honour (as well as his desire to avoid marriage), had ensured he had steered clear of innocents, and his fastidious tastes, that he gave ladies who were too loose with their favours, a wide berth. A widow – who was used to male company and missed it – was his compromise. It was meant to be a mutually beneficial experience that harmed neither party. If he felt the lady was becoming too attached, he would end things, hopefully amicably, he was not in the business of breaking hearts.

But where had his clear head and firm control of his actions been when he had, first, invited Lady Lewisham, to waltz with him at a ball where he had had no intention of dancing, and then offered to be her escort on a journey that he really should not dally on? He found himself faintly amused when she put on her prim and proper face or when she attempted his godmother's trick of cowing someone into obedience with a haughty manner, almost as if she were trying on different roles for a play, however, his objectivity and control were unimpeded. But when her feelings were engaged, and she started to talk passionately about a subject she was interested in, or when she was simply enjoying herself as she had been at the ball – her eyes lit up like emerald beacons that beckoned a man hither and halted all rational thought for a moment. He knew from bitter experience, that it only took a moment of rash behaviour to create a landslide of unforeseen consequences.

Closing his eyes, he sighed deeply and tried not to think about the fact that, at that moment, she was lying in a bed just across the corridor from his own.

CHAPTER 5

The snow clouds that had looked so
threatening the evening before had obligingly
moved off elsewhere to drop their load and
so Sophie and Miss Trew, not wishing to run the
gauntlet of the other guests, set out early the next
morning, taking some freshly baked hot rolls to eat on
the journey. The day had a grey, sombre feel to it, not
helped by the towering cliffs that, at first, marked
either side of the road, hemming them in – the feeling
further exacerbated when they, every now and then,
passed into the gaping mouth of another grotto cut
through the rock. After leaving a particularly fine
example, they turned an extremely sharp bend and
were suddenly deafened and much startled by a violent
torrent of water hurtling down into the yawning
precipice that now marked one side of the road.

It was with some relief that they entered the small
hamlet of Isella, a poor place, mainly consisting of a
few cottages, a customs house, and a posting inn. The
feeling was to be short-lived as barely had they pulled

up outside the inn when they were approached by two indolent-looking customs officers. For some reason, they did not seem pleased with their papers. Sophie tried to argue her case, but the two men before her did not seem to comprehend a word she said. Before she quite understood what was happening, one let out a low whistle and two rough-looking men in home-spun tunics with rough clogs on their feet came running up and started to throw their baggage unceremoniously into the road.

"Lawks, my lady! Whatever are they up to?" squealed Burrows, before jumping down and giving them a piece of her mind, using language that under other circumstances would have earned her a sharp telling off, but in the present case, Sophie felt far too grateful to cavil at. Squires soon joined her, but they might as well as have been addressing one of the many large boulders they had passed on their journey, for all the effect they had.

"This is ridiculous," Sophie muttered, alighting herself.

"Stop this at once!" she ordered furiously. "I am sure our papers are quite in order and insist that you put everything back immediately!"

To her consternation she found herself completely ignored, the customs men having the temerity to turn away from her, apparently admiring the view of the mountains with rapt attention as if seeing them for the first time.

Even as she spoke, their two lackeys opened her trunk and began rifling through it.

"Here, leave my Lady's things alone, you ruffians!" screeched Burrows grabbing one of them by the arm, outraged that her careful packing was to be so disturbed. He shook her off as if she were an irritating insect, causing her to fall onto the rough road.

"You foreign, good-for-nothing bully," she cried from her prone position before bursting into tears. Squires tried to comfort her, but she rounded on him fiercely. "What use are you, you good for nothing clod-pole? Leave me alone and do something for my lady!"

Goaded into action, he stepped purposefully forward but found himself floored by a giant fist, anchored to an arm that bulged with sinew and muscle.

The sound of hoof beats cantering towards them could just be heard above the din. Sophie turned her head to see three horses approaching at an impressive rate. Two had riders, and the other seemed to be carrying their baggage. A magnificent black stallion led the way. The words she had uttered the evening before were forgotten in the rush of relief she felt as she recognised the dark hair and fine form of Sir Philip. He and the horse moved as one. She had just time to register the firm muscles that guided the great beast, (and which his serviceable leather breeches did little to hide), and that his expression was unusually forbidding before he reached them, dismounting in one fluid, graceful movement.

"Stay, Alcides," he said in a commanding tone before striding purposefully towards the two men still intent on their task.

He grabbed them roughly and banged their heads together. Grunting, they both fell swiftly to the floor.

"Sophie, get back in the carriage," Miss Trew pleaded quietly as she pointed with one shaking, outstretched finger, towards the customs men. Their attention was now entirely on the scene before them, and one had a gun pointed directly at Sir Philip, the other had a supercilious grin etched across his smug face.

Sophie gasped and felt herself begin to tremble, her treacherous limbs turning to jelly. Her instinct was to help Sir Philip, but she could not see how it could be done or bring her wayward legs under enough control to move an inch.

He looked as calm as ever, however, merely nodding towards a point beyond their shoulders. "I wouldn't if I were you," he said coolly, with quiet authority.

They had all forgotten his companion, but now turned their heads to see him still sat astride his bay gelding, a pistol held in each steady hand and a reckless grin spread across his face.

It was all the time Sir Philip required. He moved as swiftly and silently as a panther. The smug one did not see the hammer-blow coming that knocked him instantly unconscious and the other had barely time to register the occurrence before he found himself relieved of his pistol, his arm twisted painfully behind his back, and his feet almost leaving the ground as he was marched back towards the customs house.

As they disappeared inside, Sir Philip's companion approached, still mounted, guiding his horse by his knees alone, just as the two ruffians got to their feet, rubbing their heads and muttering curses under their breath.

He briefly nodded respectfully towards Sophie. "Vaughen, Sir Philip's batman, I mean groom, at your service, my lady," he said shortly before turning back towards the men.

"Put everything back as you found it!" he said menacingly, both pistols now firmly trained on them.

His character was hard to read from his weathered face – for although his countenance was not unpleasing, with lines radiating from his eyes, suggesting he was not a stranger to laughter – the deep scar that ran from just below one ear to the edge of his mouth, suggested that he was someone who was not to be trifled with.

Sophie finally found her voice, concerned that Sir Philip had not, as yet, re-appeared. "Thank you, Vaughen. Perhaps if you would lend me one of your pistols, I could oversee things here whilst you check on Sir Philip."

He did not withdraw his keen eyes from the two men busily re-packing her bags, but they crinkled with amusement. "Bless you, lass," he began, then hastily corrected himself, "I mean, my lady. Don't fret yourself. The day I have to help him sort out one fat, lazy official, is the day – god forbid – he has been given notice to quit!"

When she still did not look convinced, he added, "Believe me, Lady Lewisham, when I tell you that he would not thank me for interfering."

As at that moment, Sir Philip and the customs officer re-appeared, the question became a moot point.

They both approached her and seeing their advance, Miss Trew bravely stepped down from the carriage and stood beside her charge, all quivering indignation.

They came to a stop before them, the customs officer's face a mixture of resentment and shame. It seemed that he had suddenly re-discovered his command of English. "I am sorry for the trouble, Lady Lewisham. Having re-inspected your documents, I find them in order, and would ask you to forgive any inconvenience and feel free to be on your way."

About to answer herself, she was startled and surprised when her retiring companion took a step forward and answered for her.

"You are a disgrace to your office, sir," Miss Trew exclaimed earnestly. "How proud your mother must have been, when you attained your current position, but how do you think she would feel now if she had witnessed your recent behaviour towards two defenceless women?"

His amazed glance swivelled in her direction, taking in the pristine, if rather drab, figure before him.

"She died last year," he eventually admitted.

"How fortunate for her that she is now experiencing the joy of meeting her maker rather than witnessing the perfidy of the child of her loins!"

Sophie gasped in shock and admiration as his face twisted in embarrassment and he shifted awkwardly from foot to foot like a schoolboy caught out in some misdemeanour. "I am sorry..." he began but was mercilessly cut off, for Miss Trew had been overcome by the zeal of a believer who has the chance to spread the word of God in all his righteousness and perhaps redeem a lost soul.

"Do not try to exonerate yourself from your outrageous behaviour," Miss Trew continued like a stern governess, much to Sophie's continued amazement. "Our good Lord said, 'joy shall be in heaven over one sinner that repenteth, more than over ninety and nine just persons, which need no repentance.' Learn that lesson well and make sure you do not disgrace your name – whatever that is – or your calling further!"

To the astonishment of all and the embarrassment of Miss Trew, suddenly there were tears in his eyes, and he dropped to his knees, taking her hand in his own and weeping unashamedly all over it. She had not taken into consideration the less guarded emotions of the foreigner before she had begun her sermon.

"Control yourself, man," said Sir Philip disgusted, helping him to his feet. Then offering a brief bow in the direction of the ladies, continued, "I suggest we partake of whatever light refreshment this hostelry has to offer whilst your baggage is stowed. Go ahead, I will join you in a moment."

"An excellent suggestion," agreed the customs man, recovering his poise and eager to make amends, moving with unaccustomed alacrity towards the inn and ensuring that a private parlour and free refreshments were made available to them.

Sir Philip found both ladies still a little shocked, huddled together as if for comfort on the settle beneath the window. He was immediately followed into the chamber by a serving girl who served them a glass of wine each. Sophie took a grateful sip and tried to gather her scattered thoughts together.

"I cannot thank you enough, sir, although I admit I am at a loss to understand why we were treated so."

"Indeed, I shudder to think what may have happened if you hadn't arrived so fortuitously," added Miss Trew.

Sir Philip stood looking seriously down at them.

"Oh, nothing too grave. After an exhaustive search of your baggage, you would have been allowed to continue. At some point on your journey, however, you would have discovered that various items of value were missing."

Miss Trew gasped. "The scoundrels!"

Sir Philip smiled gently at her. "I am afraid this is one of those occasions when book-learning is an inadequate chaperone. If you had greased him in the fist, in the first place, I believe you might have avoided any unpleasantness."

Sophie, recovering some of her natural energy, pushed herself to her feet and began pacing up and down in a decidedly unladylike manner, her indignation clear.

"Oh, a bribe! How foolish of me! I should, of course, have invested in a book that informed me of when and how much I would need to bribe corrupt public officials! Oh, and let us not forget, greedy innkeepers! I suppose if I had greased the fist of that bumptious little man last evening, a free table would have miraculously become available."

She had come to a stop directly in front of Sir Philip, her eyes ablaze and her bosom heaving at the exertion. He looked distinctly unimpressed with her outburst.

"Undoubtedly. But is all this heart-burning necessary?" he said, quite harshly. "Did you not wish, how did you put it − to expand your mind and understanding? If you insist on travelling without the protection of a male relative who would already understand these things and take care of them for you, then you will have to expand your understanding in ways that you have not imagined!"

Sophie heard the censure in his tone both at her loss of composure and her ignorance and felt heat rush into her cheeks. She was relieved when she became aware of the comforting presence of Miss Trew beside her and the tension that seemed drawn between herself and Sir Philip, eased a fraction.

"Perhaps you will let us re-pay you whatever sum you were required to expend on our behalf," Miss Trew said gently.

Sir Philip's face softened as he looked down at the diminutive, little lady before him. "I believe I can stand the nonsense. You were quite remarkable, Miss Trew," he said, making her blush. "You gave him something far more valuable than mere money, you gave him the chance to redeem his behaviour and become a better man!"

"It is true, Agnes, I never knew you could be so stern, you were wonderful!" agreed Sophie.

Miss Trew smiled mistily up at Sir Philip. "You were very impressive yourself, and I am quite sure your mother would have been very proud of you!"

His smile faded, and they both felt his withdrawal. "She is also dead," he said flatly, his suddenly inscrutable countenance not inviting platitudes.

"I have already offered to act as escort to you both, and although I am not a relative as such, I feel our mutual connection to Lady Renfrew impresses some obligation on me to ensure your continuing safety. I am afraid I am not on a sight-seeing tour but have some business that I must attend to in Pisa without delay, so you must resign yourself to travelling hard for a week or so. I will be ready to leave in five minutes."

With that, he bowed and left the room. Sophie looked rebellious, but Miss Trew merely said in a matter-of-fact way, "Well, we already seemed to have jumped into the fire, my dear, so come, let us go. I do not like to disappoint you, but I confess I will feel far more comfortable with Sir Philip's escort than without it."

The scenery was at first as dramatic as that which had gone before, with bridges thrown over wild gorges, where torrents plummeted downwards into the bowels of the earth. But gradually, softer hues gentled the prospect until at last, they had a glimpse of the vast plains of Italy. Imperceptibly, the vegetation became more exuberant until they were surrounded by acres of vines, groves of olives, and generously laden fruit trees.

When they came to Lago Maggiore, whose shores were a hive of activity, dotted with towns, villas, churches and castles, Sophie fretted that they were not to be given time to explore them as Miss Starke had detailed several places of interest. The same thing happened at Milan, with Sir Philip pressing on to the smaller town of Lodi.

"I particularly wished to see the Cathedral at Milan," Sophie said wistfully. "It is one of the largest in Italy."

"We had already agreed that we could not see everything," soothed Miss Trew. "Console yourself with the reflection that Miss Starke herself suggested that the buildings there, in point of architecture, are in no way remarkable. When we reach Pisa, we will be able to dispense with Sir Philip's escort and take our time to look about us, and at least we will get there without being swindled or robbed!"

The day had been persistently gloomy with some fierce downpours, and after travelling for several hours, the sight of the city gates was a welcome relief, until Sophie realised it was past dusk and they had already been closed.

"Wonderful!" she exclaimed. "He has made our teeth rattle in our heads, travelling at a quite ridiculous pace to reach this insignificant place for no good purpose!"

Miss Trew decided to let this pass. Sophie had always studied, but she had also balanced this with vigorous exercise as she always said it allowed her thoughts and ideas to percolate somewhere in the back of the mind until they were ready to form into coherent theories. It was indeed hard on her to spend all day in the close confinement of the carriage.

"Ah, look, my dear," she said suddenly, "Sir Philip has done the trick, they are opening!"

"Of course, he has," Sophie muttered darkly. "I expect he has greased the fist of another public official! I wonder what budget he sets aside for the purpose?"

CHAPTER 6

The following day dawned fair, and Sophie, keen to be up and exploring, stood at the window watching the sky as it gradually lightened, drawing on a rose-pink cloak shot through with orange threads. Unable any longer to still the increasing desire to be out in the beautiful morning, she silently left the inn and the town; the tall walls, which had offered such a welcome embrace to tired travellers last evening, now felt like an encumbrance to be shed.

She walked out as far as the bridge that spanned the River Adda, the wide waterway that stood beside the town and leaned against the parapet, looking down at the gently murmuring waters below. She watched as they meandered around some obstacles and over others, quietly determined to continue on their way.

"It is a beautiful spot, is it not?" Sophie jumped, and Sir Philip put out a hand to lightly steady her.

"Sir Philip! Are you following me?"

He quirked an eyebrow and immediately she felt foolish, conceited even.

"Not at all, it is mere coincidence. You must share my love of early mornings, Lady Lewisham."

"I felt the need for some exercise," she explained, annoyed that she sounded slightly defensive. "We have spent so much time shut up in a carriage, you see."

Sir Philip nodded but looked a little stern. "Your need for exercise is understandable, Lady Lewisham, but it was not wise to wander out here alone."

Sophie's eyes narrowed. "I thank you for your concern, sir, but I hardly think I stand in any danger at such an hour and in such a peaceful setting." Unconsciously, she had begun tapping one little foot, and she winced as it came into contact with a sharp stone on the downward beat. Bending swiftly, she picked it up and threw it into the clear waters below.

They both watched as it briefly agitated the smooth surface before disappearing from sight.

"Even in a small, unassuming place such as this, a single event can occur, which sends out world-changing ripples," Sir Philip said quietly.

Sophie looked interested. "Oh? Did something of that nature, happen here?"

"Indeed – it is where Napoleon faced the Austrians in his first Italian campaign. The Austrians were in a strong position on one side of this bridge, yet he inspired his men to charge across it in the face of awful gun and artillery fire. It is the battle that earned him the confidence and loyalty of his men and persuaded him he was a superior general, destined for great things."

Sophie looked intrigued and surprised. "You speak almost as if you admired him!"

Sir Philip regarded her seriously. "And why not?"

For a moment Sophie was lost for words. "But you were a soldier!"

He nodded once.

"You fought against him?" she prompted.

He nodded again.

Feeling a little exasperated, she said, "Then he was your enemy, he killed people you knew and would have killed you without a thought, so how could you possibly admire someone like that?"

Sir Philip looked pensive for a moment and then smiled wryly. "The French would no doubt say the same of Wellington. Both Napoleon and Wellington were great leaders in their own ways: both could inspire and motivate their men in the face of over-whelming odds, both were usually the master of sound strategy, and both did not hesitate to put themselves in danger. The real difference between them was motiva-tion. One was driven by the need for glory, the other by duty. I intend to be driven by neither!"

"What are you driven by?" Sophie bit her lip, drawing his gaze, as she belatedly realised how personal and potentially provocative her words were.

His smile grew wider and a predatory gleam entered his eyes. Sophie felt powerless to move, even as she realised his head was moving closer to hers. Her eyes fell to his finely moulded lips a moment before they whispered against her own. He laid no hand upon her person, and it was the lightest of touches, yet when he pulled away, she found she was trembling.

"Your problem is that you see everything still in

SOPHIE

black and white," he murmured. "But as a widow, I think you will find there is a whole world of greys in-between!" He began to lower his head again, but she took a step back, snapped shut her parasol, and prodded him sharply with it.

"Oh, you – you rogue! I had just thought you might be worth getting to know after all!"

Sir Philip winced and held one hand over his heart. "Ouch! Your words are far deadlier weapons than your parasol, ma'am! If you find my boring on about military history more fascinating than my kisses, I really am losing my touch!"

"I know nothing of your touch! Nor do I wish to!" she added hastily seeing that predatory look return. "It seems you do not hold a very flattering opinion of widows, but let me make it plain to you, sir, I am not now, nor will I be, at any time in the future, interested in a, a ..."

Sir Philip leant his back upon the wooden parapet, folded his arms, and waited with apparent interest. After he had watched her flounder for a few moments, he took pity and filled in the gaps for her. "A slip on the shoulder? Carte blanche? Affaire? Dishonourable Proposal?"

Colour flared into her cheeks, and she found both her tongue and her parasol, which she used to great effect to punctuate each utterance that followed, forcing Sir Phillip to retreat before her or risk being turned into a pin-cushion. "I am an independent woman of means! It is my firm intention to stay that way! I am not interested, now, or at any time in the future, in relations with any man and with you in particular. I do not want you, I do not need you, and neither do I wish to see you again after your disgraceful behaviour! Napoleon may have won his battle at Lodi – you will not!"

On that delightful utterance, she turned smartly around and marched back in the direction of the town, her nose tilted towards the sky and her parasol back where it belonged.

Sir Philip shook with silent laughter as he watched her progress. The little termagant! He had indeed served under Wellington, and one of that man's strengths had been to know when to retreat. It was something he ought to do now, of course. But he had felt her tremble, and if he were honest, he wanted to feel it again. It was strange that a widow responded like an innocent. If it were a ploy to keep him interested, it was working – if it was not, then she was deceiving herself – the red tones in her hair, the way her emerald eyes flashed with anger, all spoke of a passionate disposition. That all that passion should be focussed on events and objects that were ancient history was a tragedy. Clearly, her experience of marriage had not been satisfactory; the age gap between his own parents had not resulted in a happy union either. A wry smile curled his lips as he acknowledged that he was some years older than her himself, but then he was not proposing marriage. *He was not proposing anything!* he reminded himself ruefully. The kiss had been rash. Ungallant even. He had promised her his protection. Sir Philip groaned: he was going to have to apologise.

Sophie's heart was beating at an alarming rate of knots as she climbed the stairs of their Hotel, not only due to the impressive rate she had maintained all the way back. Her cheeks were flushed and her eyes bright as she burst into her room.

"My dear, whatever has occurred to occasion this wild appearance?" exclaimed Miss Trew, alarmed.

"It would appear I have jumped out of the frying pan, into the fire and now into the furnace!" she said vehemently, yanking at the ribbons of her bonnet, and casting it carelessly aside. "Your Galahad is no more than a – a rake!"

Miss Trew paled at these words. "Oh, my dear, no! Do not say he has forced himself on you for I could hardly bear it!"

That gave Sophie pause for thought. She could not in all good conscience accuse him of forcing himself on her, she had seen the kiss coming after all and to her shame had made no move to avert it. Bursting into sudden tears, she shook her head. "No, he did not do that."

A little colour returned to her companion's cheeks and taking Sophie's arm, she led her to the bed. "Sit down and calm yourself, my dear, if not that, then what has happened for you to defame his character so?"

As she told the story of their meeting, Miss Trew's expression became thoughtful, her myopic gaze staring into the middle distance.

"It seems to me, my love, that you got off quite lightly. Another gentleman, finding an attractive young lady unattended, might not have found the fortitude to stop at one light kiss, parasol or no parasol!"

Sophie's jaw dropped. "Got off lightly? Aggie, you cannot deny that his behaviour was ungentlemanly, surely?"

"Perhaps not," she admitted. "But was it the behaviour of a young lady of quality to venture out alone to such a public spot?" she queried gently. "It hardly seems fair that you expect Sir Philip to follow the conventions when you so blatantly break them yourself. What is he to think? You had only needed to remain in my company, and it would not have happened, after all."

As Sophie found this unanswerable, she changed tack. "Be that as it may, I am tired of travelling every-where without seeing anything. Miss Starke mentions a church that has some remarkable works by Callisto, who was a pupil of Titian, you know. I suggest we go and view them before we are closeted up for the day once more."

Miss Trew was happy to comply with this sugges-tion. They had just donned their bonnets when following a brief knock on the door, Burrows entered carrying a letter.

Dear Lady Lewisham,

I offer my most sincere apologies for behaving in such an ungentlemanly manner. I am fully aware that I have offered your party my protection and can assure you that such a lapse of judgement will not happen again.

I would have suggested you visit the church of L'Incoronata this morning, as it boasts several impressive frescos and paintings by Callisto, but unfortunately, I have discovered it is temporarily closed for renovations due to water ingress.

As you have already visited the only other place of note, I suggest we set forward as soon as you have taken some refreshment.

Your humble servant,
Sir Philip Bray

CHAPTER 7

Forced to satisfy her curiosity by what she could glimpse from the windows of her carriage, Sophie took to studying the peasantry. She found it intriguing that those nearer the Simplon were often of fair complexion with blue eyes, and of quite a slight stature, but even as the vegetation had grown more exuberant the further south they travelled, so the people had also flourished. Sophie found the men tall, robust, and finely proportioned, but it was the women who most excited her admiration. Their dark hair and expressive black eyes were exotic, their movements earthy, yet graceful. They seemed to embody an inner life and vibrancy that shimmered in the very air around them.

However, even this occupation grew wearisome after a few more days of travelling and the rolling olive groves and rows of vines, that had, at first, delighted the eye, even acquired a sameness that she would not have believed possible not so long before.

"Thank heavens we will be in Pisa tomorrow," she

said wearily as the road curved down into a dip, surrounded on both sides by the seemingly ever-present trees in this part of the country. Sophie saw a small group of sun-kissed boys by the side of the road, waving grapes and other fruits at them. One of them began to run along beside the carriage shouting, "Uva! Uva!"

Sophie and Miss Trew exchanged a smiling glance and then on a sudden impulse, she demanded the coach be stopped, climbed down, and enjoyed a lively exchange with them, laughing when they bowed deeply and shouted, "Bella, Bella!"

Smiling widely, she curtsied to them as if they were dukes.

"Get in the carriage, NOW!" Sir Philip suddenly shouted.

Something in his tone made her comply with unusual meekness. He had been a little way ahead but now galloped back towards them with some urgency. He drew to a halt beside the carriage, throwing a pistol at Squires. "If anyone comes near, use it!" he ordered, before disappearing off into the olive groves that lined the road, Vaughen following close behind.

Alarmed, Sophie leaned out of the window to suggest the children get in the carriage with them, but they had melted away, a few bunches of dropped grapes the only sign they had ever been there. The sudden crack of a shot in the distance had both occupants of the carriage on the edge of their seats, craning their necks to try to see where it had come from, but the trees obstructed their view. Neither spoke, but clasped hands as they waited for events to unfold, their eyes never leaving the spot where Sir

Philip and Vaughen had disappeared in a cloud of dust.

They returned at a more moderate pace. Vaughen retrieved their packhorse and sent them a pitying glance before taking up a position behind the vehicle. Sir Philip approached the window of the coach and sat frowning at them for a moment, a muscle ticking in his firmly clenched jaw.

"What just happened?" Sophie asked urgently.

Eyes that were chips of ice, raked her face, sending a quiver of apprehension through her.

"What just happened, ma'am, is that you disobeyed my orders," he said harshly.

"What orders?" Sophie asked, bemused.

"I made it clear when I offered my escort, that we would only stop to break our journey at places of my choosing."

Sophie felt confused and a little hurt. Although she had not appreciated the liberties of a few days ago, she could not deny that the admiration and latent passion that had turned his eyes into endless pools that had beckoned her into their depths, had haunted her dreams. To see them look at her so scathingly now, made her feel somehow bereft, as if in losing his good opinion she had lost something important.

"Yes, you have urgent business in Pisa," she said haltingly, "and so we have accommodated your wish to travel incessantly all day, every day! I cannot see how my stopping for a few moments..."

He cut her off. "Your stopping for a few moments, at such a secluded and largely hidden spot, gave a few banditti the perfect chance they had been waiting for!"

"But my book says rumours of them are much exaggerated..."

"Damn your book!" he said, his slip of composure shocking her into silence. "We have run them off for now, but we will not stop again unless I order it!"

He made to move off. "Wait!" begged Sophie. "What about those lovely children, they may also be in danger!"

"Indeed," said Miss Trew, finally finding the courage to speak. "We cannot leave the poor lambs in the middle of nowhere when there are such rogues about."

Sir Philip let out a long, low sigh. "Why do you think those 'poor lambs' were here, in this particular spot, in the first place?"

Miss Trew looked non-plussed, but a look of chagrin crossed Sophie's face, and Sir Philip's glance gentled a fraction.

"You mean, of course, that it was their job to lure us to stop, that they were hand-in-glove with the banditti," she said slowly. "And I fell straight into their trap! I apologise."

Miss Trew's hand flew to her mouth, her eyes glinting with tears.

"I am sorry for your distress, ma'am," Sir Philip said more quietly, "but they are hardly to be blamed, after all, for they are poor and were probably offered enough reward to keep their families in comfort for some time to come."

As they travelled onwards, clouds that had been but a speck on the horizon earlier in the day, steadily closed in. Grey but with a tinge of red, they smothered the sun, casting the day into gloom. The wind also picked up, swirling dust into the air, causing the ladies to firmly shut the carriage window and Sir Philip to loosen his neckcloth enough to pull it half over his face.

When they finally broke their journey, he did not join Sophie or Miss Trew in the private parlour he acquired for their use. It was a desultory meal with Miss Trew's thoughts on the infamy of men who would corrupt poor innocent children, and Sophie trying to fathom why such an obvious withdrawal of his approval, should disturb her quite so much.

The closer they had drawn to Pisa, the more Harry had filled Sir Philip's thoughts, driving him to maintain a pace of travel that he knew must be trying for the ladies. He had been lost in them when some instinct had caused him to pause – perhaps it had been the cessation of the steady rhythm of the carriage behind or his soldier's intuition kicking in – but something had made him glance back over his shoulder.

His initial feeling had been one of irritation at the delay, followed swiftly by one of amusement as he saw Lady Lewisham cavorting happily with the ragamuffins at the side of the road. He had thoroughly agreed with their shouts of 'Bella!', for she had indeed looked beautiful and absurdly young, as she laughed with them in an unrestrained moment of happiness. A sudden twinge of something uncomfortable in the region of his heart had been quickly usurped by a feeling of tension, making him glance away into the olive groves – just at the moment when the sun had glinted brightly off something in the distance. It was a sight he had witnessed before, and his reaction was swifter than thought.

They had seen off the banditti with no great difficulty; they were after easy pickings, a warning shot that had cleanly removed the hat from one of them had settled matters. He was, however, furious with himself for the lapse in concentration that had allowed the ladies to fall behind and the subsequent unpleasantness he had subjected them to – but realised that it would be easier and quicker to deliver them safely to their destination if they were a little in awe of him. If he had dined with them and faced the inevitable look of reproach in their eyes, he would, undoubtedly, have been tempted to apologise.

He found sleep an elusive bed partner that night, the storm that had been threatening the best part of the afternoon, finally burst into life with an impressive rumble of thunder, followed soon after by a flash of lightning that seemed to rend the sky in two. The wind moaned fretfully around the corner of the building and arrows of rain bounced off the many small-paned glass windows of his room.

I hate rain! he thought, crossing his arms behind his head and staring up at the ceiling. Without warning, he was hit with a series of flashbacks that came to him unheralded and unwanted.

He and his regiment were bivouacked in a field near Waterloo. Rain lashed down, turning the field into a muddy quagmire. The struggle to stay dry was largely futile; the ground was sodden – rivulets of water poured down collars and off cuffs making any chance of sleep, negligible – particularly for him.

Whenever he closed his eyes, incongruent, vibrant, shameful images of the Duchess of Richmond's ridiculous ball intruded.

The Gordon Highlanders danced gracefully to the sound of bagpipes, candlelight glinting off the swords at their feet. The ladies clapped along, the liveliness of the dance dispelling much of the formal frigidity that often marked such affairs. Spirits were high, everyone determined not to face up to the ever-present danger of imminent battle.

Sir Philip was dancing with Miss Frances Bowles, the daughter of a very wealthy merchant. His acquaintance with her was slight, but he recognised two things about her immediately; she had a pretty face and the soul of a courtesan. When a dispatch arrived, and the word for the soldiers to slowly start withdrawing went round, she grabbed his hand and all but dragged him into a small, courtyard garden. They were in quite a compromising position when they were discovered by his good friend, Lieutenant William Hunt. He grinned sheepishly at William, assuming he had come to drag him off to the front but then saw the stunned expression on his face and the guilty one displayed by Miss Bowles.

Without saying a word, William turned on his heel and left. Miss Bowles stamped one angry little foot and descended into an energetic bout of weeping. It seemed that an announcement of her betrothal to his friend had been imminent.

"Don't you understand?" she all but screamed at him. "You were the forbidden fruit I wanted to taste before a lifetime with one man!"

"Whereas you, ma'am, were just forbidden," he

snapped coldly before hurrying to catch up with William.

Now he walked tiredly among a field of corpses; sightless eyes stared upwards, wounds gaped open as if crying out in silent distress and furtive scavengers moved silently among them, not averse to taking the clothes off their backs, the coins out of their pockets, or even the teeth out of their heads. They filled him with a rage that was both useless and futile. He began to move more quickly through the motley throng. Please God, they hadn't found Harry or William!

A blur of movement by a stand of trees to his left caught his eye. As he turned, Harry sat up among the countless dead, his blond hair streaked red and a dazed expression dimming his usually expressive eyes.

"Harry!" he called, a flood of such intense relief rushing through him that his own exhaustion was forgotten, and he managed to close the distance between them at a loping run.

Harry did not seem to hear him but just sat, staring blindly ahead. Sir Philip dropped to one knee beside him and took his dirt-streaked face in his hands. "Harry?" he said gently.

The blue eyes slowly focussed on him. "Hello, sorry old chap, I can't hear a thing! Do I know you?"

With that, he passed out again.

"Don't worry, sir, I'll help you get him back. Thought you might need a hand."

So intent had he been on searching for his friends, he had not been aware that his loyal batman had been following in his wake.

Sir Philip nodded. "We'll just move this unfortunate fellow out of the way," he said, for the first-time glancing at the poor departed soul who was draped, face down across Harry's legs.

He began to reach out his hand and then stopped short – for beneath the dirt, blood, and grime, he could see the torn coat was a Hussar uniform. With a deepening sense of foreboding, he gently turned the lifeless body and drew in a deep, painful breath, feeling a fist close around his heart as he recognised the blank countenance.

"William," he whispered softly, cradling his friend in his arms. "I'm so sorry, William!"

Even though he was bone-weary and bloodied himself, he somehow managed to stand, with William still held in his arms. Vaughen hoisted Harry over his shoulder, and together they made their slow, silent progress back across the field.

Another clap of thunder seemed to burst right over the inn, wrenching Sir Philip back to the present. He sat up with a start, covered in a light sweat. Giving up on sleep, he drew up a chair before his window to watch the storm play itself out. He had failed William in so many ways but he was damned if he was going to fail Harry!

He suddenly tensed as he heard a floorboard creak just outside his room. Grabbing the pistol he always kept beside his bed, he sat astride the chair and listened as the handle of his door slowly began to turn. The door inched open, and a dark furtive shadow moved silently into the room, holding a cudgel of some sort in front of him.

"Drop it!" growled Sir Philip.

Just then a flash of sheet lightning briefly lit up the chamber, revealing Vaughen carrying a bottle of something. "If it's all the same to you, sir, I'd rather not. I was reconnoitring this establishment when I stumbled upon a very fine cellar. This is a bottle of what they call grappa hereabouts, I thought you might like to try it."

"You fool!" Sir Philip said. "You could have been shot!"

Vaughen offered him an unrepentant grin. "You are many things, Captain, but trigger-happy ain't one of them. I have never known you to shoot the wrong man, yet! Now get a bit of this fire-water down you, it'll do you more good than being sat there looking at that gloomy scene! It's a good storm, to be sure, but I reckon we've seen more impressive ones!"

Sir Philip's lips twisted. "So we have, Vaughen, so we have. Now stop cradling that bottle as if it were your sweetheart and pass it over!"

Despite having an air of fallen splendour, Sophie thought that on first acquaintance, Pisa looked like an ancient and beautiful town. Divided by the Arno river which had a broad quay on each side, the many faded yet noble buildings that lined it, had a decaying grandeur that suggested a rich and interesting past.

The main streets were wide and excellently paved, and the bridges over the Arno were elegant and graceful. They stopped near one such structure, at the hotel L'Ussero.

"Aggie, we are finally here!" she said, alighting without delay – her pent-up excitement barely contained. She turned full circle, trying to take in everything at once, a wide smile slowly dawning. "It is as if the very buildings breathe their history!"

"It is probably the damp!" came the dry voice of Sir Philip.

Sophie turned to him her smile undimmed, any awkwardness between them forgotten in the joy of their arrival. "Oh, even if that were true, what matter? How can I thank you for your care? We have been a sad trial to you, I know, how glad you must be that having seen us safely to our destination you can carry out your business without delay."

Her openness of manner, vibrant demeanour, and glowing eyes were bewitching. She had stated nothing but the truth yet now the moment had come, he felt reluctant to leave her. Widow or not, she had all the naivety of a newly emerged schoolroom miss but none of the protection.

"It has been my honour to serve you," he smiled, bowing to them both. "You have your letter of intro-duction?"

"Indeed, it is safely tucked in my journal," she said.

He nodded. "When I have confirmed my plans, I will send you word where you can contact me if I can serve you further," he said, "but as I have some enquiries to make for my friend within, I will ensure you are comfortable before I leave."

He struck lucky first time and was directed to an old Palazzo that had been divided up into private apartments a little further along the river. It bore the signs of some neglect but a slovenly porter soon directed him to the correct door with an uninterested nod of his greasy-haired head. It was opened by a weary-looking lady with black eyes, bruised by purple shadows underneath and a full mouth that drooped at the corners, as if borne down by life's burdens. In ordinary circumstances, she must have been beautiful, but in her present ravaged and dishevelled state she looked what she was; desperate. He had no more than bowed and introduced himself when she burst into loud, unrestrained sobs.

"Lui è gravemente malato!" she cried, over and over.

It seemed that his sudden appearance had broken the final thread of her forbearance, so putting her gently aside he strode through the high-ceilinged, sparsely furnished, marble-floored reception room to the tall wooden door at the end. It gave directly onto the bedchamber, and there lay his friend. The bedcovers were tangled as if he had been thrashing in his sleep, his blond hair was dark with sweat, his face alabaster. The shutters were closed and the darkened room stank of rank sweat. After one comprehensive glance, he turned on his heel and returned to the greatly afflicted lady who had thrown herself down onto a day bed, still sobbing noisily. When his words had no effect, he dealt her one sound slap and called her name imperatively, "Maria!"

The noise ceased and she stared mutely up at him.

"Dell'acqua calda!"

Nodding she hurried over to a small wood-burning stove that crouched in one corner of the room. Returning swiftly to the bedroom, he wrenched open the shutters and threw open the doors that led onto a small balcony, letting some much needed fresh air in, and the rank smell, out.

In a matter of moments, he had stripped the sheets

from the bed and the soiled nightshirt from his friend. Just as Maria Trecoli entered with the hot water, a knock sounded at the door.

Taking the bowl and cloth she carried, he nodded for her to answer it, breathing a sigh of relief that Vaughen had been so prompt. Between them, they soon had Harry washed and in fresh laundry.

"You want me to find a doctor, sir?" asked Vaughen once they had finished.

"Immediately," confirmed Sir Philip. "One competent in dealing with malaria!"

CHAPTER 8

I n Pisa, social visits were paid in the evening and Sophie and Miss Trew wasted no time in visiting Lady Bletherington. The cameriere who admitted them conducted them through a long, narrow suite of rooms, their appearance somewhat dingy owing to each only being dimly lit by a single lamp. However, the sitting room into which they were announced, was both elegant and light, and the lady herself could not have been more welcoming.

Somewhere in her forties, she was still a handsome woman. Her light brown hair was topped with a lace cap, the only nod to her age, for her dress was fashionable, cut quite low and perhaps not quite the most flattering to a figure that was rather full. Having risen to greet her guests, she invited them to sit and sank gratefully back in her chair, hastily reading Lady Renfrew's letter. Disconcertingly, she read it under her breath, occasionally uttering a much louder exclamation, such as "Ah! Oh! or Indeed!"

"How pleased I am," she eventually declared, "that dear Lady Renfrew has guided you to me. It is a pity my daughter has gone back to England with my husband for the season for I am sure they would have liked to have met you. Her aunt is kindly bringing her out as I have been advised to stay here for my health."

Sophie murmured a polite response. Lady Bletherington did not attend to it but resumed the thread of her discourse as though it had not been interrupted.

"We have quite a community of English here, you know, but it is always a delight when we get some new blood to liven us all up! And you are interested in antiquity, delightful! You will, of course, visit the Campo Santo and the Cathedral with its extraordinary bell tower and then you must tell me what you think of them! Then there is the opera, I am myself going tomorrow and beg you and Miss Trew will join me! I have a box, you know."

Before Sophie could get a word of thanks out, she rushed on – hardly pausing to draw breath. "And then, every so often I hold an evening salon, you will enjoy that, I know. I will hold one in honour of your arrival, it will be the perfect opportunity for you to meet other congenial persons who are interested in literature, classical antiquity, and the fine arts! Byron is here in Pisa, did you know? Although he has not yet graced us with his company at any of my select little gatherings."

By the time a somewhat stunned Sophie had thanked her kind hostess for her generous invitations, the proper length of a first visit was up, and so they took their leave.

"I wonder what Lady Renfrew wrote in that

letter?" she mused. "For once Lady Bletherington had read about me, it appeared that there was no need to hear anything from me! Not that she was not good-natured and all kindness."

Miss Trew smiled, amused. "She is probably lonely, my dear, garrulous people often are – she has perhaps not quite got used to the absence of her husband and daughter. Your lending her your company will in some way recompense her for her kindness in taking you under her wing a little."

In respect of architectural splendours, the guide books assured her that Pisa could not be compared with Florence, but as Sophie had no experience yet of the latter, she could not help being more than pleased with the former. The Cathedral, its famous leaning bell tower, the Baptistery, and the Campo Santo would individually have been impressive, but together they were breathtaking. The sunlight reflecting off acres of white marble was blinding, however, and once the overall impression of magnificence had been appreciated, they discovered it was best to only look at a small segment of these glorious edifices, at a time.

The bell tower, an elegant building, leaned at an angle that defied gravity and could not fail to please. The Cathedral also did not disappoint: it was built on a scale that was both magnificent and awe-inspiring, home to over seventy lofty columns and adorned by many alters, some designed by Michelangelo. The Baptistry, however, was on a more manageable scale; its interior resembling an ancient temple. Sophie was drawn to the pulpit, whose marble columns and impressively carved reliefs were the work of Niccolo

Pisano. In particular, her eyes were repeatedly drawn to the statue that represented the Christian virtue of fortitude. It was a beautiful example of the classical revival – the naked statue designed on classical lines held a lion cub on his left shoulder, clearly referencing Hercules.

"He is beautiful, isn't he?" Sophie breathed, her eyes wide with admiration.

"Indeed," agreed Miss Trew and then stifled an unexpected giggle. Sophie looked enquiringly at her as she struggled to retrieve her usually calm demeanour. "I'm s-sorry," she whispered shakily, "but I was just thinking that your mother may have been right when she suggested I was not a fit companion for you, as I was just imagining her reaction if she were here looking at these 'indecent bits of old stone'!"

That set them both off and they had to hastily leave lest their laughter be taken for a lack of appreciation of this place of reverence or worse, a ridiculously missish reaction to seeing a naked statue!

It was the Campo Santo which affected them most, however; gothic marble cloisters with delicate traceried windows housed fine examples of Roman sarcophagi and in the galleries, many frescoes dating from the fourteenth and fifteenth centuries impressed them with their scale and execution.

They found themselves both fascinated and repelled by those that illustrated *The Triumph of Death*. Their subject matter was not easy to look upon – it was to be expected that they would be instructional in character – but the details of death and desolation were unlike anything they had seen before. Depicted as an old woman with long white hair, bat wings and claws in the place of hands and feet, the terrifying figure of death hovered over a scene where various corpses were amassed, their souls being drawn from their mouths by devils or angels depending on their ultimate destination. It effectively dampened any desire to laugh, and it was in a thoughtful frame of mind that they returned to their hotel.

Vaughen did not fail in his objective but returned with a Doctor Johnson, who was enjoying a sabbatical from his profession in order to enjoy the rumoured delights of the continent. He had run him to ground at the hotel L'Ussero.

"I thought it might be better to have someone who understood the constitution of the Englishman," he said to Sir Philip.

Doctor Johnson was a distinguished looking gentleman somewhere in his fifties. He had intelligent light-grey eyes, a shock of thick white hair, formidable side-whiskers, and a pair of bushy eyebrows that were at present drawn together in a rather peevish expression. He did not appear to appreciate being the object of Vaughen's careful selection, especially as he had been interrupted at his dinner. He was quite red in the face due to the pace at which he had been unceremoniously marched by someone he considered to look quite disreputable, and the state of the building he entered did not encourage him to think he would be well imbursed for his troubles.

However, one glance at the formidable countenance of Sir Philip silenced the many and varied objections he had been about to make on the manner and haste of his procurement. After listening to a halting description in broken English of Harry's recent symptoms by Maria and inspecting Harry for himself, he agreed that Malaria was the likely cause.

"Fortunately for you, I provided myself with a plentiful supply of sulphate of quinine before setting out. It should reduce the fever and sweating within a week. He is likely to have a sore head so keep up cold applications to his temples. I am here for another week or so, so if there is no improvement, you may send a note to the hotel."

He left in a more cheerful frame of mind, having been more than amply rewarded for his efforts.

Sophie was looking forward to her first opera and insisted that Miss Trew overcome her natural reticence to put herself forward and accompany her.

"For I do not know anyone and rely on your presence and support to bolster my confidence," she explained. Although this was true, she was also quietly determined that her dear Aggie, would enjoy all the opportunities Pisa had to offer.

Lady Bletherington duly collected them, accompanied by a young relative, her nephew Mr Maddock, who having completed his university education, was enjoying a little grand tour before applying to one of the Inns of Court, to become a barrister. He wore his wavy hair slightly long and had a rather careless way with a cravat. His demeanour was aloof, his brow often frowning, and his conversation erratic, largely consisting of what he thought were witty or satirical interjections, which were made with a strange curl of his lip. Sophie was just wondering if he was suffering from some sort of tic when Lady Bletherington leaned towards her.

"He is a big admirer of Byron," she confided in a whisper. "Writes reams of awful poetry!"

The truth of this statement was made apparent when his fitful attention suddenly became fixed on a box on the other side of the theatre. Leaving Miss Trew to enjoy the meandering flow of Lady Bletherington's conversation, she followed the line of his gaze and observed a dark-haired man with a high forehead and pallid countenance. His full lips had a sneering look about them. This, she assumed, was the man himself. She had heard him called handsome but could not agree although even from this distance she could sense something of his impressive aura. Although he seemed to hold himself aloof from the others in his box, preferring to scan the theatre below, he somehow drew the eye, making his guests fade into the background.

"And on that cheek, and o'er that brow, So soft, so calm, yet eloquent, The smiles that win, the tints that glow, but tell of days in goodness spent," Mr Maddock suddenly sighed, tragically.

"Ha!" exclaimed Lady Bletherington, nodding at the lady in Byron's box, whose red-gold hair and blue eyes were strikingly pretty, and whose extremely low-cut silk gown revealed fine rounded arms and a generous bosom. "How any of her days can be said to be spent in goodness when she left her husband to be Byron's mistress is beyond me! That's what happens when girls barely out of the schoolroom are married to men old enough to be their father! She is pretty enough I suppose but unfortunately suffers from being rather short in the leg, everybody says so."

Colouring, Sophie said, "*She Walks in Beauty* is not typical of his work, but I must admit I enjoyed the sentiment that beauty comes from within as well as without."

But Mr Maddock was not attending, and Sophie realised that his gaze was now fixed on the stage. There was a sense of barely repressed excitement and impatience about him as he waited for the performance to begin.

"So, what do you think of the great man?" asked Lady Bletherington. "It is true he looks a trifle gloomy just now, but then he has just lost his daughter, poor soul!"

It was just as well the curtain went up at that moment, for Sophie found she could not sympathise with a man who deserted the poor mother when she was increasing, denied her access to her own daughter, and then left the child to die alone in a nunnery at the tender age of five.

It was Rossini's opera of Otello. Sophie found herself entranced from the first. The energy of the performances and the quality of the acting outshone her expectations. In particular, the soulful singing and heartfelt rendition of the voluptuously beautiful leading lady playing Desdemona was spellbinding. With hair and eyes as dark as midnight, smooth pale skin and ruby lips, she brought her character to life with a passionate interpretation of the role, that was filled with drama and expression.

As the spectacle reached its tragic conclusion, she found herself rapidly blinking to dispel the tears that had suddenly filled her eyes.

"Did you enjoy it, Agnes?" she said quietly.

"I found the singing most superior and the performance moving."

A finely dressed gentleman had entered their box and was bowing elegantly over Lady Bletherington's hand, enquiring politely about her health and her family.

His entrance had a startling effect on Mr Maddock who jerked suddenly to his feet, offered only the slightest of bows, mumbled something unintelligible under his breath, and left the box.

"Oh, oh dear," said Lady Bletherington a little flustered. "He is probably overcome, poor lamb, although it is the second time he has come so one would have thought he would know what to expect. Never mind, Lady Lewisham, Miss Trew, let me introduce my good friend, Count Maldolo."

Tall with dark eyes, he greeted them both with a dignified reserve that was pleasing.

"And how have you enjoyed your experience of the opera?" he asked in perfect English.

Sophie expressed her enthusiasm fully and unreservedly earning her a wide smile, which showed to advantage his even teeth, which flashed white against his tanned skin.

"It is refreshing to hear an opinion expressed with such intelligent vivacity," he said. "I also enjoyed it,

Giselda Sirena is a rare talent who captivates all who see her. Although I fear your fellow countryman, Lord Byron did not share our view as he disappeared after the first act!"

Sophie thought she heard a slight sneer in his voice and was glad when he continued, for she did not know how to answer.

"I think only someone native to the country where opera was born can fully express the range of emotions necessary for such a performance."

"You were going to tell me what you thought of the Campo Santo, Lady Lewisham," Lady Bletherington interrupted, eager to edge her way back into the conversation. "I always think..."

What she always thought was to remain a mystery as Count Maldolo, perhaps used to her ways, interrupted.

"Yes, please, Lady Lewisham, I would be most interested in your observations."

Miss Trew unobtrusively moved her chair a little closer to Lady Bletherington and leant towards her.

Sophie mentioned the frescoes to him. "They were very well executed," she said, "and I suppose the pre-occupation of death in what is, after all a cemetery is understandable, yet they held a disturbing quality that spoke to something within me that I cannot quite explain..." she trailed off, not quite able to effectively voice the unsettled feeling that had remained with her since their visit. "Do you know the paintings?" she asked.

He nodded. "Of course. You must not feel disturbed because you feel something you do not fully understand. All good art should have such an effect on a person with sensibility and an enquiring mind. A guide book will speak to you of the pre-occupation with death at a time when plague was rife – it will try to tell you what to think by placing it firmly in its own historical and religious context – but for me this is missing the point; you could just as well glean those facts from a dry history book. Surely the role of all good writing or art is to speak to something within us, even it is only a half-formed thought or feeling. Something beyond the obvious. What I see or feel when I look at those paintings, will differ widely from your view, because we differ widely in our experience of the world – neither of our feelings will, however, be correct or incorrect."

"It is interesting that death is personified as half-demon, half-woman," she said, realising that this had been bothering her.

The count merely laughed. "Ah – but Eve tempted Adam astray and so introduced sin into the world! A woman opened the door to the devil, therefore is it so surprising that one might also represent him?"

Sophie wrinkled her brow in consideration of his opinion for a moment. "Did not Adam also have free will? Is it not a weakness to put the blame for our failings on another because we are tempted, rather than accept that we chose to succumb to temptation?" she countered, blinking away the sudden vision of a certain kiss she had tried very hard to forget.

"Indeed," agreed Miss Trew. "It is infinitely easier to decry and expose the sins of others than to correct our own."

The count bowed. "I cannot deny your wisdom, Miss Trew."

Sophie found herself approving of him, both the elevation of his mind and the gentleness of his manner were very agreeable. He soon took his leave, and Lady Bletherington could talk of nothing else but him all the way back to their hotel.

"He showed you a considerable compliment in his attentions, Lady Lewisham, for he is a considerable Patron of the Arts and is an important person hereabouts. He has a villa somewhere in the countryside, I have never been, you understand, but I have heard that he has some impressive works by the Florentine artists..."

Sir Philip was not enjoying such a convivial evening. Harry's fever had mounted, and he was raving – uttering various inchoate phrases – however, two names were decipherable and were repeatedly and sometimes desperately uttered; William and Philip. Whatever troubled him clearly harked back to that fateful day in June 1815.

Sir Philip added another cold compress to his fevered brow, murmuring, "Peace, Harry, I am here."

His voice seemed to reach him, and for a moment he opened his eyes, gazing wildly about. "No fault!" he cried before closing them again and sinking into a more settled rest.

"Seems he's sorely troubled by something," said Vaughen, coming quietly into the room, carrying a one-pot stew he had created over the wood-burning stove.

He laid it down on the small table that lay against

one wall of the chamber. "It's been a while since I've cooked your supper, sir, but I don't think you'll find I've lost my touch being as I had access to a much wider range of fresh local produce than has, at times, been the case!"

"Still no sign of Maria?" he asked.

After the doctor had visited, he had taken her to one side and thanked her for her unremitting care of his friend. When he had handed her the generous purse sent by Lady Treleven, she had broken down into noisy sobs once again. Indeed, she was so over-wrought she seemed to have an inexhaustible flow of them and so he had sent her home, with instructions to rest and not return until she felt more the thing.

Vaughen gave him a wry smile. "I took it upon myself to make a few enquiries," he admitted. "It seems that the Trecolis were in a spot of bother, sir, pockets quite to let. They seem to have left town in a hurry rather than put the dibs back in tune!"

Sir Philip's lips twisted dryly. "Ah, I see."

"I don't suppose as she had much choice, sir, if it was the will of her father," Vaughen said generously.

"Perhaps not," Sir Philip acknowledged. "But as we have received no word or letter for Harry, I must assume she did not care enough to write one."

Vaughen knew better than to continue the subject; his master was fiercely loyal to those he considered his friends.

"And the ladies?" he enquired after a moment, in an off-hand manner, as if it were a passing thought.

"Gone to the opera, sir, though why anyone would want to listen to that infernal warbling is a mystery to me."

Sir Philip nodded absently. "Keep your ear to the ground, Vaughen. If she gets into any trouble, she will in all probability be too stubborn to ask for help."

Vaughen grinned and began to clear away the pots. "You can rely on me, sir."

CHAPTER 9

Lady Bletherington's assertion that Sophie would enjoy her salon proved to be far from accurate. She found a small group of English ladies who were none of them distinguished by any remarkable understanding. Mr Maddock was the only gentleman present but made no effort to converse, preferring to strike an interesting pose against the fireplace and gaze off into the middle distance as if lost in deep thought.

Their hostess, having just received a copy of The Literary Gazette, tried to open a discussion on the merits of L.E.L's latest poem, 'Sappho'. However, it appeared that she could not render what her imagination compelled her to say, with any clarity, leaving the unfortunate but accurate impression that she did not entirely understand what she endeavoured to make intelligible to others. After a tangled speech which referred to the pain of loving not one but two men who did not return the lady's passion and most probably did not deserve it either – (though how you could fall in love at the sound of a voice, she did not know) – and the compassion one must feel for someone driven to suicide whilst at the same time condemning such an act as selfish, cowardly and ungodly, she trailed off into an uncharacteristic silence.

Sophie had not as yet acquainted herself with Miss Landon's poem and so could not come to her rescue. She noticed the satirical glances and smiles that passed amongst Lady Bletherington's guests and felt annoyed that Mr Maddock, who might, if he had any real literary pretensions have stepped into the breach, had now positioned himself as far away from the guests as possible but very near to a bottle of wine, from which he was replenishing his glass with remarkable and increasing frequency.

Rather than consider the pain of unrequited love or compare her verse to other representations of Sappho, they preferred to discuss the recent revelation that the poet was a woman and the likelihood of the poem being autobiographical, and if so, to whom the poet might be referring as rumour had it she was increasing.

She was forced to conclude that they had come merely to listen to – or spread themselves – malicious gossip. At least she was on her guard when she suddenly found herself the object of their barely veiled interest and speculation and was forced to parry impertinent enquiries into her age, deceased husband and income.

"I hear you and Miss Trew are travelling without a male companion," said one of the ladies. Lady

Montrose wore a rich dress of purple with a matching dyed feather in her hair. She was a handsome woman, and her eyes shone with a sort of malignant intelligence. "How very...brave you are!"

"Is Italy such a dangerous place?" countered Sophie with icy politeness, refusing to give fuel to the fire that would blaze if she shared the experiences that Sir Philip had rescued her from.

"Not generally no," the lady said, "but one widowed so tragically young and in the possession of a fortune, cannot be too careful! If you feel you need it, you may come to me for advice."

Sophie cast a quick glance at Lady Bletherington whose tongue had clearly been wagging and saw that she had at least the grace to look a little shame-faced.

"Indeed?" parried Sophie. "And what is it, exactly, that I must be careful of? Is it perhaps something unfortunate that you have experienced?"

Lady Montrose, on the shady side of thirty, looked a little haughty. "Experienced, of course, not! However, if you think that all the young gentleman currently on the grand tour are here merely for the history, you are sadly mistaken!"

"I am not sure exactly to what you are referring, Lady Montrose, but as the only gentlemen I have met here are Mr Maddock and Count Maldolo, who seemed a very elegant, restrained gentleman, I hope I have nothing to fear."

"Ah, yes," she said with a small smile that did not quite reach her bird-keen eyes. "Lady Bletherington mentioned that the count had seemed very pleased with you. His manners are indeed very becoming, and he has a handsome countenance does he not?"

"I cannot say that I formed an opinion on the matter, he must be above forty after all," Sophie replied. "But it seemed to me that he had a pleasing intellect."

When she proved such a disappointing source of information, they inevitably turned their attention to Byron.

"It is no wonder he is looking so pale, I hear he is at present living solely on a diet of vegetables!" one lady began.

From there it was a small step to tearing apart the character of Byron's mistress, Countess Teresa Guiccioli, whilst all the time pretending to admire her fortitude in putting up with the whims and moods of her capricious lover.

Feigning a headache, Sophie made an early departure much to the relief of Miss Trew.

"I declare, I have rarely been more disappointed," Sophie said as soon as they were in the carriage. "I had expected an evening of rational conversation."

"It is a shame, my dear," concurred Miss Trew, "and I must own myself astonished that Lady Renfrew, who has such a fine intellect herself, should have recommended to you a lady who may have a kind heart, but has remarkably little sense or reason."

"Perhaps she had no other acquaintance presently residing here and thought that Lady Bletherington would be better than no acquaintance at all," she said, unwilling to hear any criticism of the lady to whom she had taken to so readily.

"Indeed, it can be the only explanation," agreed Miss Trew faintly.

By the following morning, they had begun to see

the more amusing aspects of their evening but had tacitly agreed that Lady Bletherington could be of very little practical use to them. As they lingered over breakfast, a card was delivered to their private sitting room. Count Maldolo had come to call.

His appearance was immaculate; his buff coloured coat fitting his broad shoulders perfectly and his linen, crisp and white. Showing an elegant leg to the ladies, he bowed and apologised profusely for intruding on them so early.

"But it occurred to me after our interesting conversation at the opera, Lady Lewisham, that although you have witnessed some of the architectural splendours Pisa has to offer, you may not have experienced some of the beautiful scenery we have, that perhaps only a local, could show you. I have come to see if you and Miss Trew would like to drive out with me before the day becomes too warm."

"That sounds delightful, but we are not quite ready..." Sophie began.

"It is of no moment," said the count. "I will await you downstairs, take your time."

By the time Burrows had attired her mistress in a simple Pomona green carriage dress of cambric muslin and chip hat with matching ribbons and parasol, twenty minutes had passed.

"Very becoming," approved Miss Trew, herself plainly attired in a light beige pelisse and straw bonnet.

"I am sorry to have been so long," Sophie said ruffled, "but Burrows will never be satisfied until I am as neat as a pin."

"Quite right," Miss Trew approved.

Count Maldolo showed no signs of impatience,

however, merely giving her an approving glance. "I am impressed that you could be ready in less than half an hour," he admitted.

"It is a minor improvement," Sophie said with a wry smile.

"I am afraid it may be a bit of a squeeze," he apologised, handing Sophie first into the gig. "But this way we can easily explore some of the smaller tracks that would be impossible to navigate with a larger carriage."

It proved a very pleasant morning. The count led them a winding way through a country of enchanting scenery where the fecund plains, dominated by the vines and olives, were at times interrupted by sun-baked fields of golden wheat. Every cottage they passed had a small garden filled with an abundance of vegetables. He took them through gentle glades of shade and past small meadows filled with a profusion of wildflowers, pointing out pomegranates and junipers, rosehips and the sweet-smelling sambuca.

"What is that lady doing?" Miss Trew asked interested, when she saw an old lady dressed in black making her way around the bases of the trees and a small stone wall that separated them from the road, every now and then bending low to pull something from the earth and place it in her roughly woven basket.

"She will be picking wild asparagus or fennel, mushrooms or nepitella, a sort of wild mint," he explained seriously. "There are many poor people here, but for those with wisdom the land provides plenty."

As they made their way back into Pisa, they passed

quite near the residence of Lady Bletherington. Perhaps it was this circumstance that made Count Maldolo enquire if they had attended her salon last evening.

"Yes," Sophie said carefully, unwilling to denigrate Lady Bletherington in any way. "But it was not as interesting as I had hoped. I was surprised to find no local ladies present."

"Ah," said the count with a small amused smile. "But the adventurous English like to travel all this way, and then gather together like homesick children. They have already experienced Italy in their minds through literature, paintings, and travel guides and so find confirmation of their opinions or disappointment everywhere."

"You are cynical, sir!" Sophie said, surprised.

"Perhaps. I have too often witnessed discussions at these salons that merely regurgitate whole passages that have been read in books with no reflection or recourse to their own imaginations. They freely give of their opinions without feeling the merits they praise or the defects they censure. But you, Lady Lewisham, impressed me when you strove to understand the feelings your imagination could not quite grasp after having seen the frescoes in the Campo Santo."

Sophie felt a desire to defend her countrymen and women, but her experiences of the evening before and the flattery to her intellect made her struggle to find an adequate defence.

"And do Italian ladies hold salons?" asked Miss Trew quietly.

"Not any that I would grace with the name of

lady," he said. "My daughter is very knowledgeable," he admitted. "But she would not choose to use in company knowledge which she has acquired in private, a lady may read much, but it is sometimes wiser to conceal all."

"I thought Italy would be more enlightened," Sophie said surprised. "But it is not so very different from home in this respect."

"Is knowledge any less valuable to an individual if it is not brought out into a public discussion where it is often misunderstood, argued over endlessly and then dismissed?"

Even as he spoke, they pulled up outside the hotel just as Doctor Johnson rushed out of the door, his black bag in hand, followed swiftly by Vaughen. They had several times exchanged greetings with the doctor, and Sophie felt a sudden twinge of alarm.

"Vaughen," she called as the count politely helped her descend from the gig. "Is anything amiss? Is Sir Philip ill?"

"No, my lady," he said hastily. "But the friend he came to see is and he is concerned for him. It hasn't helped that the lady who was caring for him has disappeared and Sir Philip insists on looking after him single-handed. I daresay lack of sleep is making him fret, so excuse me, but we must be on our way."

"Wait!" Sophie said as he turned away. "Is it far?"

"No, ma'am."

"We will also come, then. It may be that we can help in some way."

"I'm not sure..." he began, but Sophie impatiently cut him short.

"Nonsense, it is the least we can do when he has taken such good care of us."

Sophie turned to take her leave of Count Maldolo. He took her hand and looked at her intently for a moment. "This Sir Philip," he said. "He is a friend of yours?"

"Yes, he escorted us part of the way here," she confirmed.

The count bowed. "Then I will send you the directions of my own doctor also."

"Perhaps my services will not be required, after all," grumbled Doctor Johnson, clearly offended.

Miss Trew smiled gently at him. "Oh, Count Maldolo is just being polite, I am sure you are very accomplished, sir. Come," she said taking his arm, "we must not keep Sir Philip waiting, for I am sure he must be very anxious to have disturbed you."

Sophie hid a smile at Miss Trew's masterful handling of the situation; she was finding herself respecting her companion's judgement more every day. She supposed as a vicar's daughter she had been used to dealing with her father's parishioners.

The count watched them go, a small frown creasing his brow. He suddenly cracked his whip driving off at a spanking pace, causing an unwary gentleman to hastily jump out of his way.

Sir Philip was indeed anxious, Harry's fever had continued unabated even with the quinine, and although he had occasionally opened his eyes and been persuaded to drink, he had not shown even a flicker of recognition when he had gazed straight at his old friend.

He had left the door ajar and so did not immediately perceive that he had extra visitors. As Doctor Johnson entered the room, he briefly shook his hand before turning back towards the bed as Harry cried out something unintelligible.

"His head seems to be causing him much discomfort, he keeps clutching it and thrashing from side to side. He must not die!" he said imperatively. "I do not care what it costs or how it is to be done, but you must bring him back to me!"

Sophie and Miss Trew, who had hung back in the main reception room, exchanged a speaking glance, for it was impossible to miss the depth of affection in which he held his friend or the agony of worry he was in. Sophie could not help wondering what it would be like to have someone feel such a deep affection for her that they would do anything to keep her close.

Sir Philip strode into the room a moment later, running a hand through his dark locks. Judging by their disarranged appearance, it was an act he had repeated many times before. He wore no coat or cravat, and his shirt was open at the neck, revealing the strong column of his throat. He looked tired, dishevelled, and vulnerable, yet incredibly virile at the same time. He stopped short when he saw his guests.

"Ladies," he said surprised and then bowed, swiftly recovering his poise. "How may I be of service to you?"

Ignoring the fact that her heart had begun to beat a trifle faster, Sophie stepped forward. "We require no service from you, Sir Philip, but on the contrary are here to offer our own. And by the look of you, not a moment too soon."

He coloured slightly. "I am sorry you find me so disarranged, I am unprepared for visitors."

"It is of no moment," she said. "It is we who should apologise for having burst in upon you unannounced but having heard of your friend's indisposition we came with all haste to see what we could do."

He rested his hooded gaze on her for a long moment, taking in the clean crispness of her gown; the colour emphasised her emerald eyes – she looked like a fresh spring flower. The idea of her spending tedious hours mopping his friend's fevered brow did not sit well. "I thank you for your kind consideration," he finally said, "but the sickroom is no place for such a fresh daisy as yourself, Lady Lewisham."

"Is that so?" she challenged, tilting up her chin slightly. "Perhaps you have forgotten that I was married to a man who was much older than me and sick for some time before he died? Or did you think that I would leave all his care to his attendants whilst I occupied myself shopping for fripperies?"

Perhaps fortunately, Doctor Johnson, having finished his inspection of the invalid, joined them at that moment saving Sir Philip from the necessity of making a reply, for he did not have the energy or appetite for an argument.

He looked solemn. "Things are indeed at the critical point. The disease has gone too long unchecked, and so the symptoms are strong. We must up his dose of quinine in the short term for if he falls into a coma, there is nothing else to be done."

Sir Philip looked grim. "We must not allow that to happen!"

"I could bleed him..."

"No!" Sir Philip snapped. "I have witnessed too many soldiers die after such a procedure. I believe it drains the spirit and he needs all the energy he can muster if he is to fight this, his hardest battle."

"Daisies!" said Miss Trew suddenly.

All eyes swivelled in her direction at the unexpected utterance.

"Doctor Johnson, when Count Maldolo was driving us through the countryside this morning, I am sure I saw some feverfew. If I could make an infusion of the plant, surely it would help with the fever and the headaches, in particular?"

"Indeed, it could," he agreed. "At least it will do no harm and it may do some good."

Having not been brought up to an idle life, Miss Trew warmed to a useful role. Turning to Sir Philip decisively she said, "Your care and concern for your friend whilst admirable, cannot be maintained if you take so little care of yourself, sir. You not only look dishevelled but half-deranged into the bargain! We will indeed collect some feverfew and make it up, but we will share the care of ... your friend."

"Harry," he said. "Viscount Treleven."

Although naturally shy and retiring when taken out of her natural milieu, Miss Trew had indeed been used to offering succour to the needy in her father's parish and found her competence for managing difficult situations overtaking her usual reticence when dealing with the gentry. Glancing at the bundle of blankets folded neatly on the day bed, she continued undaunted. "And I see no good reason for you to be sleeping rough in this lodging, it is far from ideal and in the present circumstances, quite unserviceable. I shall book rooms for you and Lord Treleven at the hotel, where you will find it easier to access both the esteemed Doctor and the basic comforts necessary to your wellbeing, as well as making it less difficult for us to offer our assistance."

Doctor Johnson observed Miss Trew with some respect. "You speak a great deal of sense, ma'am," he said approvingly. "I will happily administer the required dose myself and judge when it is time to lessen it again, for too much for too long will also be injurious to Lord Treleven's health."

His natural inclination towards privacy together with his anxiety over his friend had prevented Sir Philip thinking with a clear head, but now he saw all the advantages of this proposal. A slow smile eased some of the worry that etched his brow and Sir Philip took Miss Trew's hand and kissed it lightly. "Did I not say you were a remarkable woman?" he said. "But as for sharing the care, I would not presume to intrude on your time...."

"Our time is ours to do with as we choose," interjected Sophie, decisively. "I will send my carriage so you can transport Lord Treleven easily to the hotel and we will help you care for him, for I think you will find that even a daisy, whilst preferring the sun, is hardy enough to cope with inclement conditions when necessary."

Sir Philip bowed low over her hand, his eyes never leaving hers. "You are all consideration, Lady Lewisham. I fear I did not do justice to you when I compared you to a common daisy; you are more like an orchid, rare and beautiful."

"And hard to cultivate," she added dryly, her antipathy to flattery automatically kicking in. "One kind act does not an orchid make! I prefer to be a daisy."

CHAPTER 10

Lord Treleven was moved in remarkably little time and now finding himself surrounded by an unexpected network of support, Sir Philip allowed Vaughen to persuade him that he should take a truckle bed in Harry's room.

"For if you are going to tell me that I am incapable of caring for him, all I can say is your memory must be failing you, for if you have forgotten the times I have tended to you..."

"Enough!" said Sir Philip with a lopsided smile, clasping him on the shoulder. "It is not my lack of faith in you that has driven me, and well you know it! Now, I will leave Harry to your tender ministrations whilst I bathe, for I have agreed to dine with the ladies."

Doctor Johnson also joined them for dinner. Between them, they came up with a schedule which would not be too demanding on the ladies but would allow Sir Philip time to rest and exercise.

"I will agree to this arrangement but only when Harry has shown significant improvement," he said.

"And on the understanding, that if he becomes lucid and wishes to speak to me, I will be fetched immediately."

After dinner, both gentlemen excused themselves. Sophie and Miss Trew settled by the fire; Sophie with a book, Miss Trew with some embroidery. Sophie was aware of a strange sensation of comfort at knowing Sir Philip was under the same roof. As this feeling ran contrary to her desire for independence, she tried to analyse it and come up with some rational explanation for it. She had not got very far with this endeavour when they were interrupted. Two Italian ladies were admitted to the parlour – one young and pretty with thick, glossy dark hair and a shy demeanour – the other much older and quite stern-looking. The hair that peeped beneath her hat was pure white, and she had small hard current-like eyes. The Marchesa Rossanna D'Orza introduced herself and her niece.

"I believe you have already met Contessina Isotta's father, Count Maldolo?"

Sophie smiled widely. "Oh, how wonderful to meet you both! Contessina Isotta, your father spoke very fondly of you. I am delighted you have come to visit!"

The young lady offered a small smile in return and said in a low musical voice, "My brother also speaks of you with respect, Lady Lewisham."

"We cannot stay," said the marchesa briskly, refusing to be seated, "but would like to invite you to a small breakfast at our villa outside town tomorrow. It is the Villa Maldolo, ask anyone, and they will direct you. Come at ten, before the day gets too warm to enjoy the gardens."

Hardly waiting for a reply, she then swept regally

out of the room again. Contessina Isotta again smiled but said nothing, following in her wake with a quiet grace.

Sophie stood looking after them for a long moment. She felt undecided as to her own desires in the matter, feeling that they had rather been ordered than invited. However, she could not deny that she had a strong inclination to visit the villa and see the impressive collection of art Lady Bletherington had mentioned, as well as to get to know Contessina Isotta a little better.

"Do you think we should go?" Sophie finally said to Miss Trew. "We have promised to help with Lord Treleven, after all."

Miss Trew looked unruffled and re-applied her needle to her work. "Well, my dear, as Sir Philip made it quite plain that he would not accept our assistance until the viscount is much improved, I do not see the harm. That is, of course, if you wish to go. If you do not, you could always develop the headache," she said with a small smile.

Sophie laughed aloud at her friend. "Then we shall go, I own that I am a little intrigued to see if the elegance of his villa will match the elegance of his person."

Burrows dressed Sophie with her usual care in a round robe of jaconet muslin under an open pelisse of pale grey sarsnet. Her satin straw hat boasted three rows of matching grey ribbon around the crown. A few rich ringlets peeped from beneath it.

"There," Burrows said satisfied. "You're pretty as a picture, my lady."

"Thank you, Burrows," she smiled. "As usual your

taste is impeccable."

"It wouldn't matter how impeccable my taste was if I didn't have such good material to work with," she grinned. "I once worked for a lady who always looked like a pudding no matter what I did!"

Sophie was still laughing when she stepped onto the landing just as Sir Philip came out of his room further along the corridor, dressed for riding. Her laughter drew a smile from him, and he bowed briefly before crossing the distance between them in a few long strides. He already looked less care-worn, and his appearance was immaculate.

"You look charming, Lady Lewisham," he said lightly.

Sophie dropped a brief curtsey and dimpled prettily. "Why, thank you, kind sir. I have it on the best authority, my maid's, that I do not, at least, look like a pudding!"

His smile widened, and his eyes crinkled in amusement, for the first time she noticed the fine laughter lines that radiated from them and thought how much they suited him.

"As you are going out, can I hope that Lord Treleven is perhaps a little improved?"

"His fever is not quite as virulent, and he spent a more restful night, so I am cautiously optimistic that the increased dose of quinine has begun to work. I am loath to leave him for long, however, I need some exercise and fresh air. You are going out yourself ma'am?"

Sophie told him of the kind invitation they had received. "It will be interesting to get an insight into the manners and customs of some local people rather than just sight-seeing."

"Yes, a place is not defined solely by its art or the stones with which it was built," he agreed. "I will enquire the way and escort you as I am going for a ride anyway, perhaps Miss Trew might show me the feverfew she prescribed for Viscount Treleven for his head is still bothering him."

As he led them past the gentle murmur of a limpid stream, a wild meadow spread before them covered with the daisy-like feverfew, the white and yellow of the flowers occasionally broken by a splash of red as wild poppies sprang up amongst them.

Sir Philip left Alcides to drink from the stream and found himself drawn by a sweet, fragrant scent to the fringe of the meadow. It reminded him of something that nudged the edge of his memory. He came to a stop in front of a wild myrtle shrub. Its deep green leaves contrasted pleasingly with the many pure white flowers that decorated it, a plethora of golden-tipped stamen erupting from their centres like delicate starbursts.

Sophie left her parasol in the carriage and at the last moment also stripped off her kid gloves lest they get covered in green stains. Curious as to what had caught Sir Philip's attention, she wandered over to him.

"Oh, they are beautiful," she said, bending low to breathe deeply of their heady scent.

It was her scent, he realised, only magnified by the huge array of blooms. From this moment on, he would always associate her with the myrtle. Acting on impulse, he broke off a spray and handed it to her. In doing so, he disturbed a butterfly the colour of lapis lazuli. It fluttered agitatedly into the air, alighted on the flowers she held for a moment, and then darted away on the breeze.

Smiling widely at him, she slipped it through a button hole on her pelisse.

"The Greeks knew the plant as Myrtos and associated it with Aphrodite," he said softly. "The Romans, as Myrtus and associated it with Venus. Ovid describes her rising from the sea, holding a sprig."

"Of course," said Sophie. "I have read of it somewhere. Thank you. You have brought the myth alive for me!"

Sir Philip smiled wryly. It was typical of her to be more interested in the classical overtones of the plant, whereas the usual innocent society maiden would have blushed and fluttered her lashes – aware of the romantic ones – and the less innocent would have been more interested in the aphrodisiac properties associated with it!

"We had better help Miss Trew gather some specimens," he murmured dryly. "Or she will read us a lecture on the iniquities of idleness!"

"And she would be quite right to do so!" Sophie said, turning and making her way into the meadow.

The feel of the warm sun on her back and the gentle breeze rippling through her hair was delicious, bringing a soft smile to her lips. She began to hum an old nursery tune as she moved amongst the feverfew. Leaving the tiny white flowers, she bent low to pick the feathery leaves that gave off a strong citrus-like aroma. The sweet sound of birdsong filled the air, and she thought that it felt like a long time since she had so thoroughly enjoyed the calming effects of nature. Realising that despite her wide-brimmed bonnet the sun was now full on her face, she swivelled, still low to the ground and reached for the next nearest plant. Her pale, smooth hand brushed against another, much larger and stronger than her own.

Feeling a fizz of energy shoot like lightning up her arm and through her body, she gasped and raised two wide luminous eyes. She felt as if time itself had stalled; the scent of the meadow and the sound of birdsong faded away until only they remained, and she found herself drawn towards and lost within Sir Philip's ocean-deep gaze.

"I think we have enough leaves to last us for quite some time," came the gentle but clear voice of Miss Trew.

Sir Philip sprang upright immediately and offered his hand to help Sophie to her feet. She did not take it but slowly straightened as if in a half-dream and turned towards the calm voice that slowly filtered through her stunned senses, grounding her and enabling her to breathe once more.

Miss Trew took her arm and led her back towards their carriage at the same time filling the silence with her gentle chatter.

It was not long before they turned a bend in the road and were confronted by two large gates that had been thrown open in anticipation of their arrival. A long avenue lined with cypress trees led towards the villa, a loggia ran along the front of the upper floor supported by a series of classical looking columns. Spread out in front of them were impressive gardens.

As they made their way towards the villa, they admired the well-kept ornamental parterres which were occasionally interrupted by invitingly shaded paths, some lined with classical statuary. Nearer the villa, the soft breeze carried a fragrant smell. They saw that here, the neatly clipped box-hedges framed beds filled with herbs. In the centre, a three-tiered fountain was displayed, topped by a graceful nymph and to either side were two fierce lions from whose mouths water also spouted.

They pulled up beside an elaborate balustraded front, which was reached by two opposing sets of steps and gave entrance to the villa. Count Maldolo was waiting for them there. Sir Philip did not dismount but gave the count an appraising stare before briefly nodding. The count also took his time surveying his unexpected visitor before running lightly down the steps and returning the acknowledgement by the briefest inclination of his head.

Sophie felt the strange tension between the two men and hastily introduced them.

"Sir Philip was kind enough to show us the way," she explained, glancing from one to the other.

Neither broke their stare.

"Thank you for seeing the ladies safely here, please stay and refresh yourself," the count eventually said – politely enough – but his countenance remained grave and offered little encouragement.

"Thank you for your kind offer, but I cannot stay," Sir Philip replied, somewhat tersely.

"Ah, your friend is still sick?"

"Yes, so if you will excuse me," he said, offering a brief bow in the general direction of all before abruptly wheeling his horse about and cantering back down the avenue.

"I would have escorted you myself if I had thought

you would have had any difficulty finding the way," the count said a trifle stiffly, unable to keep a hint of disapproval from his tone. "But come, the ladies are ready for you."

Sophie was surprised when instead of mounting the steps to the villa, he led them to a side garden. It was delightful, bordered by pots of lemon and orange trees, its central focus was a large shaded pergola draped with vines, with tubs of rosemary and lavender at its base. Underneath a long table was filled with a great variety of cakes, bread, fruits, ham, and figs.

The marchesa and Contessina Isotta both stood and offered them a small bow. Dropping a light curtsey, Sophie smiled. "It is nice to see you both again and how wonderful that we can partake of our meal in such a beautiful and fragrant setting."

"Ladies, I have a little business to attend to but will join you later," said the count, bowing briefly before disappearing back around the side of the villa.

An awkward silence followed, and Sophie found that she did not know quite how to break it. The contessina was dressed rather plainly in a cotton print dress with a warn shawl draped around her shoulders although the day was already warm. She kept her hands demurely folded in her lap, her smooth face expressionless, and her eyes downcast.

An old servant dressed in faded livery, who looked like he should have been retired years ago served coffee and then withdrew. Then and only then did the marchesa speak, proceeding to a diligent cross-examination of Sophie's birth, marriage, and the reasons which had brought her so far from her own country.

"You were fortunate that your family managed

such an advantageous marriage for you," she said.

"But I am surprised that they would approve of you travelling such a distance with only one female chaperone at such a young age."

"But then I am a widow and not dependent on their approval," Sophie said quietly.

"But surely you would not go against your families' wishes?" she probed.

"I would certainly never wish to behave in a way of which they would disapprove," Sophie hedged, sending Miss Trew a rather desperate glance.

Miss Trew knew her duty and began to address a series of questions on the medicinal qualities of the various herbs she had seen, drawing the marchesa's attention away from her employer.

"You must forgive my aunt," Contessina Isotta said, her voice barely more than a whisper. "Things are different here, and she is somewhat old-fashioned in her views."

Sophie felt sorry for the girl, who barely seemed to dare utter a word in her aunt's presence. By gentle questioning, she managed to discover that she had not long returned from the nunnery where she had been educated, and it was hoped that a marriage for her would soon be arranged.

Sophie smiled. "And who is the lucky man?"

The contessina merely shrugged, but her soft mouth drooped sadly. "I hardly know, some marchese from an ancient family, like your husband he is much older than me. I will not get to meet him until the contract has been signed."

Sophie was a little shocked, although a similar arrangement had been made for her, she could have refused, and she had certainly met her future husband on more than one occasion before she had accepted his offer.

She had no opportunity to probe further as at that moment the count returned.

"If you have finished, might I suggest a turn about the gardens?" he suggested.

The marchesa declined, so Sophie and the count went ahead down the narrow walkways, with Miss Trew and Contessina Isotta following behind. They came to a shady walkway where a series of classical statues were placed at even intervals; all were toga-clad ladies who were looking over their shoulders towards them.

"They are beautiful," said Sophie pausing to run her hand over one.

The count regarded her thoughtfully for a moment. "In their way, but you are more so."

Sophie felt something in herself recoil at the cool delivery of his words. "Please," she said, putting out a hand as if to ward them off.

But the count took her gloved hand in his own and bent to brush his lips against it. "How is it that you can admire and comment on the beauty that surrounds you, yet you would disparage those who find within themselves a similar sentiment when they look upon your form? You dismiss it immediately as artifice and empty of all true sentiment, and where this is true, you do no harm and maybe even some good. But where the feeling is truly felt you wound the bearer of it and in doing so diminish your own worth!"

Sophie had felt no depth of sentiment in his words and neither did she wish to. She had the feeling that he viewed her as another object he would like to add to his collection. She had, at first, been drawn to the elegance of his person and the gentleness of his manners; he had always displayed a dignified reserve that in no way threatened her and that he had not uttered meaningless nothings to her had been to his advantage. Now she realised that behind that reserve lay a lack of any human warmth that was chilling.

"I have no wish to wound you or any man," she said. "If beauty I have, it is through none of my doing. I admire these statues for their form, yes, but I would rather be admired for a virtue that I have cultivated, for some act or achievement that is worthy of merit, than for merely possessing the face and form that God gave me."

The count released her hand and offered her a small bow. "Forgive me if I spoke out of turn. I meant no disrespect."

Miss Trew and Contessina Isotta had at last caught up with them. Sophie noticed that the young girl sent an anxious glance from beneath her lashes in the direction of her father. Sophie took her arm and turned back towards the house but found it difficult to draw any conversation out of the contessina. Each enquiry had her sending a nervous glance over her shoulder reminding Sophie of the row of statues so recently observed. The formal gardens, where every tree and border were clipped suddenly felt oppressive, and she realised that she had preferred the more natural, wild beauty of the meadow.

As they approached the villa, Sophie thanked Count Maldolo for his hospitality and asked for her coach to be summoned. Any feelings of disappointment she might have felt at not having seen the rumoured treasures within the villa were superseded by the desire to avoid any opportunity for another tête-à-tête with him.

She pondered on what she had observed as they made their way back to town.

"That poor girl hardly dares to breathe without her father or aunt's permission," said Sophie.

"She has indeed been brought up very strictly," agreed Miss Trew. "I believe it is the custom to keep the girls close until they are married so that no whisper of scandal can attach to their name."

"It is more than that," Sophie said. "I could not help but feel that there was a well of sadness within her and I did not hear one kind word addressed to her. I hope her marchese proves to be as kind and generous as Edward proved to be."

As soon as Sir Philip was through the gates, he let Alcides stretch into a gallop. He had not liked leaving Lady Lewisham and Miss Trew just as he had not liked leaving Harry. He generally trusted his judgement and he had not liked Count Maldolo. There had been no warmth in his offer of hospitality, and he had felt the underlying resentment at his presence that had bristled through the man. That he had some interest in Lady Lewisham, he had no doubt – that she was unaware of it – he also had no doubt. The feeling that he had left a lamb to the slaughter niggled at him and only the knowledge that Miss Trew would watch over her had enabled him to take his leave. He had done so with alacrity as the desire to ruffle the count's feathers had been very tempting. In all truth, he would have liked to have pushed him up against the wall and threatened him with all manner of unpleasant things if he dared to so much as breathe too close to Lady Lewisham.

He groaned. He was in trouble. When she had been happily moving through the flowers in the meadow, humming a sweet melody, utterly uncon-scious of her grace and beauty, he had felt himself drawn to her like a moth to a flame. When she had turned so suddenly and their hands had met, skin on skin, that flame had burned in her eyes, sending a dry heat through him, igniting a desire that whispered to him to lay her down among the daisies and sip her nectar. Thank heaven for Miss Trew! One calmly uttered, commonplace phrase had been more effective than a douche of cold water. Much more worrying though, was the wave of fierce protectiveness that had possessed him as he had watched her return slowly to herself. The urge to sweep her up into his arms and carry her somewhere, anywhere he knew she would be safe from anyone who might try to corrupt the inno-cence that he had felt within her, even as he had felt her desire burst into life at that brief touch. Widow or not, she was that rare thing, an innocent temptress. Only a snake would try to take advantage of that, only marriage would do for Sophie, Lady Lewisham, but marriage was something neither of them wished for.

Harry, he must concentrate on Harry. He would make sure that Lady Treleven would know the happi-ness of being reunited with a son whom she loved unconditionally, even as his own mother had loved him.

CHAPTER 11

That evening Lady Bletherington came to call with the reluctant Mr Maddock in tow. Dressed as carelessly as usual, he bowed politely enough and then went and sat on the window seat and stared down into the street below – as if whatever was going on there, was bound to be more interesting than anything the ladies might have to say.

"My dears," Lady Bletherington said as soon as she was through the door, "how cosy this room is, no wonder you are tempted to stay in by the fire, these old grand palazzos are all very well but not always very comfortable. Now tell me everything. How have you been spending your time in this delightful city?"

When told of their invitation to visit the Marchesa D'Orza and Contessina Isotta, she looked amazed but perhaps more surprising was Mr Maddock's reaction. Rising from his perch in the window, he came and sat next to his relative, his eyes fixed rather unnervingly on Sophie.

"You were honoured indeed to be invited to their estate for it is not as it is at home, my dear. Italians prefer to visit at the opera or theatre rather than entertain at their homes. The count must be very impressed with you. Yes, indeed, very impressed," she trailed off, already writing in her mind the letter that she would send to Lady Renfrew as she was sure to be interested in such a promising event.

Sophie felt a twinge of irritation; she had purposefully not mentioned Count Maldolo, unwilling to give Lady Bletherington food for the gossip that she knew would be spread around her circle without delay – not because she was malicious – but because she could not help herself.

"Tell me, what did you make of the marchesa? She is very proud is she not? It is said she was very much in love in her youth with some count or other, and there was an arrangement between the families that they would wed, but he all but left her at the altar. Apparently, he fled afterwards for fear of terrible reprisals! She was then married to an ancient marchese who made her miserable, and when the present count's wife died, she came to live with him."

"I know nothing of this," said Sophie, wondering why, if it were true, she was complicit in forcing Isotta into such a similar situation. "She was certainly very reserved. Contessina Isotta seemed a very gentle creature."

Mr Maddock sighed deeply at the words.

"Her beauty is divine, her bearing gentle, her brow pure, her gaze soft..." he trailed off.

"You know her?" Sophie said surprised. "It seemed to me that she was kept very close." She certainly could not imagine someone of Mr Maddock's stamp being let anywhere near her.

"I saw her at the opera the other night," he said dreamily. "The Maldolo box is next to Byron's. But you are right," he said bitterly, "there is no way of getting near her, she is guarded as if she is a prisoner, and he her jailor!"

"Surely, you exaggerate, sir," said Miss Trew gently. "Would a jailor take his daughter to the opera? Perhaps she is more like a precious jewel, that may be occasionally displayed but must be kept safe at all times."

Mr Maddock ran a hand through his long, limp locks and got swiftly to his feet. "Pah! She is displayed only as her beauty reflects well on the owner of it! Like all his other treasures! He thinks as highly of himself as if he were a Medici. Come, aunt," he said with uncharacteristic firmness. "We must not take any more of these good ladies' time, we have other visits to make, remember?"

Sophie was amazed that Lady Bletherington responded with such alacrity to his unusual display of decisiveness, laying her hand on his arm and smiling warmly up at him. "How right you are, dear, where would I be without you?"

Sophie though relieved at their departure, was conscious of a nagging worry. "Aggie," she said slowly, "do I imagine it, or did you think that Mr Maddock knew more about the family than he should have?"

"Well, my dear," said Miss Trew thoughtfully, "if the poor boy is forced to escort his aunt everywhere and retreats into the background regularly, I should think he hears all sorts of odd bits of gossip that could lead him to draw a quite false picture of the situation."

Sophie smiled warmly at her friend, just because he had echoed some of her own feelings after her visit, (feelings that on reflection seemed out of proportion and exaggerated), did not mean he had formed them at first hand. "You are right, of course, but he spoke of Isotta with such reverence that I find it hard to imagine he has not somehow met her."

"Ah, but unlike you, my dear, he is of a romantic disposition, or thinks he is which amounts to the same thing! The beauty that is witnessed from afar will never be tainted by the realisation that she has a shrill voice, freckles or bad teeth..."

Sophie started to giggle. "Oh, stop it, Aggie, for you know the contessina suffers from none of these terrible afflictions!"

A timid knock at the door brought them to their senses. Recognising the knock, Miss Trew bent over the fire, removed the kettle she had placed there, and filled a cup with its steaming water. A pungent, bitter smell filled the room as Sophie opened the door.

Doctor Johnson came in smiling warmly at the ladies. He seemed to enjoy sitting with them for half an hour in the evening, almost as if for that short time he could imagine he was enjoying the comforts of his own home.

"How is our patient?" enquired Miss Trew.

The Doctor's smile widened. "His fever becomes less virulent by the hour and his head does seem to be improving."

"How kind of you to administer to him so carefully and patiently," she said, real admiration in her warm tones. "I have just prepared another infusion, I will just pop it up to him."

"Let me," said Sophie, taking the steaming cup from her hands. "You entertain our visitor. I will not be above a moment."

A gentle smile curved her lips. She was reasonably sure that Doctor Johnson's admiration for Miss Trew was also at the heart of the visits. He was far too proper a gentleman to take advantage of her good nature, however, and so she felt no qualms in leaving her with him. They usually fell into a discussion of various herbal remedies versus more traditional ones, and although they often disagreed, it was in such a gentle manner that you would have had to be listening very carefully to have noticed.

Sophie did not knock; she did not wish to either disturb the patient or his watcher if they were asleep. As she peeped around the door, she saw Sir Philip was in his shirtsleeves, a book in his hand and his eyes firmly fixed on his friend. The viscount was still and pale, but his breathing was quiet and regular.

"How is Lord Treleven?" Sophie said in a whisper, coming fully into the room. "I have brought another one of Miss Trew's infusions."

Sir Philip moved as if to stand, but Sophie waved him back. "Please, don't. The sickroom is no place for such formality."

Sir Philip's lips twisted into a smile. "He is sleeping so peacefully, I am not sure I should wake him."

As Sophie glanced towards the patient, he opened his eyes and looked straight at her, his gaze clear.

"If that potion tastes as disgusting as it smells, you can take it away again!" he said with a weak grin.

"Harry, do you know who I am?" Sir Philip said, surging to his feet.

A twinkle came into his eyes. "Hello, old chap. Had to wake up – couldn't stand any more of that twaddle you were reading to me. I would have thought my letter made it clear that I didn't think much of that Byron fellow. Happy to see you of course, but just at this moment I'm more interested in the vision of loveliness hovering at the end of my bed as if she had seen a ghost."

Sophie's dimples peeped out as she offered him a small curtsey. "Do not be mistaken by outward appearances, my lord," she said, "for I am determined you will partake of this potion, however disgusting it may smell."

"You are clearly a witch, and I have not the strength to argue," said Lord Treleven, holding out a recalcitrant hand that refused to do the dictates of his will, but shook alarmingly.

"Here, let me," said Sophie, gently lifting the cup to his lips and offering him a small sip. When he wrinkled his nose, she murmured, "Just a little bit more, my lord."

As he drank, her eyes lifted and locked with Sir Philip's. There was a wealth of relief and something else she could not quite identify in his glance.

"Give me a hand, will you, Philip?" said the viscount, trying to push himself up into a more upright sitting position. "I'm weak as a kitten!"

Between them, they raised him without difficulty and Sophie adjusted the pillows behind him with a proficiency that suggested it was not the first time she had taken part in such a manoeuvre.

"That is hardly surprising, sir, when you have hardly swallowed a mouthful of food for the better part of a week. I will ask the kitchens to send up a chicken broth," Sophie said firmly.

The viscount closed his eyes wearily, but a small grin still played around his mouth. "I can hardly wait! Where is Maria?"

Sophie withdrew discreetly as Sir Philip perched on the edge of his friend's bed.

"She's flown the coop," he said gently, before explaining the situation.

Harry closed his eyes as he listened. They sprang open at the mention of his mother, and a small laugh shook him.

"Thank heaven she did not accompany you. Maria had a dramatic flair that would not have sat well with her."

"If you mean she was fond of hysterics, I know!"

"Poor Maria! She deserved the reward, you know, she looked after me even after my own funds ran out. Her father ran a café, but unfortunately took part in the more serious gambling sessions that went on in private upstairs, unsuccessfully as it seems!" Harry's head sank back against his pillows as if the very act of speaking had drained what little energy he possessed.

"And my father?" he asked softly.

"He was thrown from his horse and broke his neck not long after you left," Sir Philip said gently.

Harry's jaw clenched, and his hands curled into fists. "My poor mother," he finally said.

"Yes, she did not take it well and has only recently come out of seclusion. The sooner I get you home, the better," said Sir Philip.

Harry's eyes shot open again. "Home?"

"We have much to discuss, Harry, but it can all wait until you are much stronger. The only significant things you need to know are – Worthington did not die, and I intend to return you to your mother as soon as possible."

Harry closed his eyes again and the sigh that he slowly exhaled, seemed dragged up from the depths of his soul. "Worthington did not die!" he whispered. "Yes, take me home, old chap. Take me home!"

Sir Philip watched his friend fall back into a deep sleep and realised that his jaw was rigid with tension. Slowly massaging it with his hand, he came to a sudden decision. He withdrew a leather pouch from his discarded coat's pocket, strode over to the window that looked out onto the courtyard below, threw it open, and let out a low whistle.

Within moments, Vaughen appeared. Sir Philip threw the pouch down to him, not at all surprised when he caught it without a fumble. "Get yourself to Leghorn and in the morning book us passage on the first sea-worthy vessel that will take us home."

Vaughen grinned up at him. "Will do, sir. Good English air is just what his lordship needs!"

They were in luck, an English merchant vessel, The Minerva, was due to leave for London in two days.

"But do you think Lord Treleven is in any fit state to be moved by sea?" Miss Trew said in her gentle way when Sir Philip broke the news to them.

"He will cope with it far better than a land journey, which would jolt his emaciated form and aching head quite horribly. He is used to sailing and the voyage will give me time to feed him up a bit, for I dare not hand him over to his mother in his present condition!"

"But what if he suffers another relapse?" said Sophie, aware of a sinking sensation in the pit of her stomach.

Sir Philip turned to Doctor Johnson with a wry smile. "This is where I hope I can persuade you to accompany us, sir. I will, of course, pay your passage and you may name your price for your time, services and the early end to your tour."

Doctor Johnson looked torn – although he had been able to afford to come on this trip, he was by no means so well off that he could easily dismiss both the payment and privilege of serving the gentry. Also, he had come to a slow realisation recently that he was indeed missing the comforts of his home. He suspected that he might be a little too old and set in his ways to be experiencing his first grand tour. Involuntarily, his eyes turned towards Miss Trew.

She smiled gently at him. "It would be a prudent move indeed, for I am quite certain the Doctor's presence must make all the difference to the continued improvement and management of Lord Treleven's condition."

Finding he could not bear to see himself diminished in this good lady's eyes, he had agreed to it before he had quite realised what he had done.

Sir Philip bowed first to Miss Trew and then Sophie. "Your willingness to offer support to myself and Lord Treleven will not be quickly forgotten. Do you head to Florence, soon?"

Sophie forced words past the strange lump that had formed in her throat and said with a small smile,

"We were becoming quite a cosy party. Count Maldolo would condemn us as a party of home-sick English, so perhaps it is for the best!"

Sir Philip's brow puckered slightly. "Is his opinion of such importance to you?"

Sophie laughed and shook her head. "Only in that, I would not wish to prove him right!"

Sir Philip took her hand for a moment. "I have spent a large portion of my life avoiding my own home and country, but now that I have found Harry, I wish for nothing more than to be back there. I will admit to both a feeling of homesickness and uneasiness at leaving you behind. If you do wish to return, you only need say..."

Sophie withdrew her hand from his gentle grasp and clasped it firmly behind her back because for a mad instant she had been tempted to curl her fingers closer around his and concede that there was nothing she would like more than to return with him. Not because she had tired of Italy, but because she felt that she would be less disappointed with the loss of the sights Florence and Rome had to offer than with the prospect of his absence. This thought frightened her more than a little. *You must continue to develop your character and independence.* These had almost been Edward's last words of advice to her and she had faced the disapproval of her family and the discomforts and dangers of her journey in an effort to follow them. Was she really ready to give up that independence and entrust her character to a gentleman who though a loyal friend to Lord Treleven and a charming and capable companion to her and Miss Trew, was still a confirmed bachelor and known womaniser? She could not see that becoming any man's mistress could help her develop either her character or independence and as Sir Philip had assured her that he did not intend to be driven by duty, she could not imagine that he had any other motivation in mind.

"If you had seen how I fared on the relatively short crossing to France, you would be grateful that I will not be accompanying you. At least this way, Doctor Johnson will be able to concentrate all his efforts on Lord Treleven! If you would like to borrow my carriage to take him to the port, consider it at your disposal."

Sir Philip looked stern for a moment before bowing and offering a crooked smile. "That won't be necessary. I will be taking Harry down to the port by canal, tomorrow. I hope you enjoy the rest of your visit. If you run into any trouble send word to the British Consulate in Florence."

Sophie raised her chin slightly at this. "So, you still think that we are incapable of looking after ourselves?"

Sir Philip's grin widened. "I may have been mistaken when I compared you to an orchid, after all, you are as prickly as a cactus! Lay your prickles, Lady Lewisham, for I shall allow that you are more than capable of adapting to the conditions in which you find yourself."

Deciding that the hotel would be a little flat after the departure of Sir Philip and Doctor Johnson, the ladies were also packed and ready to leave the following morning.

Harry was carried down in a chair, too weak and dizzy yet to walk that far but too proud to allow Sir Philip to carry him.

"Ah, there you are, my sorceress!" he said, spying Sophie stood amongst her luggage. "You can be no less for you silenced the army of tiny hammers that were attacking my poor skull! For such a service, I will be eternally grateful!"

Sophie smiled as she saw his eyes were glowing with a sort of feverish anticipation. He was obviously pleased and excited to be going home. She shuddered as she briefly contemplated the weeks at sea he would have to endure first.

"It is rather my companion, Miss Trew, whom you should thank, sir, for both the inspiration and the recipe for the potion came from her."

Sophie's opinion of him grew as he immediately turned his attention to Miss Trew, his gallantry undiminished.

"Miss Trew, you are an angel. I would ask you to come closer, please."

Smiling at Lord Treleven as if he were an amusing child, she approached him and offered him a small curtsy. He beckoned her closer as if he wanted to impart something of a private nature to her, but when she bent forward, he kissed her soft cheek as if she had been his old nurse.

"Thank you."

To Sophie's surprise, rather than becoming flustered, she merely smiled indulgently down at him. "Well, by rights, it is Doctor Johnson you should be thanking, for I think your recovery is largely down to him."

"Well, if we have all finished praising everybody else, it is time we were going." Sir Philip was brisk and business-like.

Sophie handed him the letter she had stayed up late composing. Knowing how sharp Lady Renfrew's observation skills were, she had found it surprisingly difficult to write. She had been very careful not to refer to Sir Philip too regularly or too warmly and she had struggled to mention Lady Bletherington at all without making her appear the foolish creature she undoubtedly was. To relieve her feelings somewhat, she had sacrificed Mr Maddock, and sketched for Lady Renfrew an image of his outward appearance and erratic behaviour that would, she hoped, amuse her. And then she had come to her visit to the Maldolo estate; she could not omit it as she was very sure that Lady Bletherington would also be writing to Lady Renfrew and would be sure to mention it and invest it with a significance that it did not merit. She saw no reason to keep from her, the awkward scene he had initiated or her unequivocal response to it. Her finished letter was no masterpiece of the epistolary art, but she hoped, conveyed a coherent, lively account of their experiences so far.

Their boat was waiting on the canal, just outside the hotel. Lord Treleven made as if to stand, but his legs buckled.

"Damn your pride," muttered Sir Philip, picking him up as if weighed no more than a small child and striding off with a final nod to the ladies.

"When you return to England, please feel free to call on me at any time," Doctor Johnson said, colouring slightly as he pressed his card into Miss Trew's hand, before hurrying off after them.

Both ladies were unaware of the other's long sigh as they watched the barge slowly disappear around a bend in the river. Their carriage swept out onto the road at that point, snapping them out of it. They had agreed they must pay a call on Lady Bletherington on their way out of town and Sophie unexpectedly found herself looking forward to the empty stream of her chatter, hoping that it would fill the emotional void which she had felt suddenly close around her.

They knew something was amiss as soon as Lady Bletherington's cameriere admitted them. He had always been silent and distant before, so Sophie was unprepared when he suddenly clutched her arm, pulling her along, excitedly saying, 'The Inglese mi'lady has turned into a donna Italiana!"

At first bemused by this odd comment, all became clear as they were shown into her sitting room and found Lady Bletherington half reclining on a sofa, her lace cap wildly askew, weeping and wailing in quite an abandoned manner. She was attended only by her maid, who stood by uselessly wringing her hands.

Miss Trew was immediately before her, waving her small vinaigrette beneath her nose. When this failed to make her more coherent, Sophie retrieved a small vase from a nearby table, unceremoniously threw the wilting flowers on the floor, and dashed the remaining discoloured water over the poor, afflicted lady.

Her maid gasped audibly, but the effect was immediate. The smell and the slime from the liquid caused Lady Bletherington to cease her shrieking as she found it necessary to hold her breath whilst she frantically scrubbed at her face with her sodden handkerchief.

Sophie turned to the maid. "Stop standing there gawking and go and fetch her ladyship a glass of wine!"

As she scurried from the room, Sophie perched precariously on the small amount of sofa remaining and took her hands.

"I am sorry, ma'am, but if we are to help you with whatever has caused this distress, you must calm yourself."

Lady Bletherington shuddered and took a great gulp of air but gradually contained her emotions until only the odd, small sob escaped her. The wine seemed to restore her further, and she managed to sit up a little.

"It is my poor Bertie," she finally said. "You must help, Lady Lewisham, he has gone!"

"Bertie?" Sophie asked bemused, trying to recall if Lady Bletherington owned a dog by that name, it seemed the sort of name one might give to a dog.

"Mr Maddock," she said a trifle impatiently. "He has become quite infatuated with the daughter of Count Maldolo! He imagines her persecuted and himself in the role of her noble rescuer!"

Sophie felt quite stunned. "But where would he get such an idea?"

Lady Bletherington looked a little uncomfortable. "Oh, I don't know. Where do romantic young men get any of their ideas? Some ridiculous poem? Some hypothetical discussion?"

Miss Trew looked askance at the latter suggestion. "And has he been witness to such a discussion?"

A pink tinge infused Lady Bletherington's pale cheeks. "Lady Montrose has quite a wit," she admitted. "She likes to weave amusing tales around some of the Italian characters who hold themselves aloof from us, no one seems to know quite what happened to his first wife after all," she broke off at Miss Trew's amazed stare. "But it is all nonsense, everybody knows it is all nonsense!"

"Clearly not everybody!" Sophie said drily.

This brought Lady Bletherington back to the matter-in-hand.

"Oh, my dear girl! You are the very person! I fear he has gone to abduct her! With only honourable intentions of course! You must go after him...explain to the count...do something, anything! When I think of what he might do to my poor nephew!"

"Lady Bletherington, you cannot consider it an honourable act to attempt to remove a gently reared girl from her home!" Miss Trew protested. "It is wicked, quite wicked!"

"And most unlikely," interjected Sophie. "How would he achieve it? He can hardly drive up to the villa unnoticed! Even if he could, I can hardly imagine Contessina Isotta would agree to such a thing! She has been strictly reared in a convent after all!"

"So was Byron's mistress," Lady Bletherington said tearfully, "and look where that has ended! Please, help me. I am sure poor Lady Renfrew would wish it."

That had Sophie's full attention for she would never have ascribed such an adjective to that particular lady. "Poor Lady Renfrew?"

Lady Bletherington suddenly covered her mouth with her hand as if to cram the words just spoken, back in.

"I am sworn to secrecy," she whispered. "Forget I said anything!"

For such a loquacious lady she suddenly became

remarkably clam-like, a sly look in her watery eyes. Nothing Sophie said had any effect.

"Oh all right," she finally muttered, exasperated. "I will go to the Maldolo villa but only on the condition that you will immediately tell me what it is you wish to keep from me concerning Lady Renfrew."

Clearly, that had been what Lady Bletherington had been waiting to hear for her lips sprang open on the utterance.

"Thank you, Lady Lewisham. I am sorry to report that I have indeed heard from Lady Renfrew and she is mortally sick. Influenza! You know how it is with these persons with unusually strong constitutions, they are hardly ever ill, but when they are...and of course, she is not as young as she used to be. Her letter was very affecting, but she insisted I say nothing to you or her godson, who I believe is also in Pisa. Although as he has not seen fit to visit me, it is hardly likely that I could say anything to him."

Her suddenly peevish tone was quite lost on Sophie who had gone very still and pale. She had a sudden image of Lady Renfrew, alone and unattended apart from her servants. She knew this was unlikely as although she was a childless widow, she had plenty of friends and acquaintances. She had been the only one of Edward's relations he had seemed to have any fondness for, and she was not surprised for they shared the same irreverent sense of humour and acute understanding.

Sophie's troubled eyes turned towards Miss Trew. "I think we should go to her," she finally said.

"I agree, my dear," Miss Trew said calmly. "We

must also send word to Sir Philip, for he will want to know, I am sure."

"We will do better than that," Sophie said decisively. "We shall join him on his journey!"

Miss Trew looked a little worried at this proclamation. "But, my dear, you suffer horribly with seasickness."

"Oh, what matter?" she said impatiently. "Lady Renfrew was so kind to us. Indeed, I felt more at home in her house than I ever did in my own!"

"Don't forget my poor Bertie," interjected Lady Bletherington.

"The villa is not far out of our way to Leghorn," Sophie assured her. "But we will not be returning, so send a servant with us who can return to you with any news."

"My dear, how will we explain our uninvited visit?" asked Miss Trew, once they were shut up in their carriage once more.

"We are merely taking our leave," said Sophie firmly, "for if we find any sign of 'poor Bertie', I will own myself amazed!"

She was mistaken. As the carriage approached the house, they heard a piercing scream. Glancing up towards the source, they saw Contessina Isotta leaning precariously over the parapet that framed the loggia on the first floor. Mr Maddock and Count Maldolo were struggling together in front of the steps. The count, the taller of the two, pushed Mr Maddock roughly away causing his unbound hair to fall in front of his face. As he impatiently pushed it out of his eyes, he received a punishing right hook to his jaw that sent him sprawling in the gravel. Count Maldolo then picked up his whip which had fallen to the ground in their struggle, and with a practised flick of his wrist cracked it ominously above the prostrate Mr Maddock who began to scramble backwards as fast as he could on his elbows.

Sophie had seen enough, jumping down from the carriage she perhaps unwisely placed herself between the two gentlemen.

"Stop this at once, sir. I cannot believe you would attack a man who is already down!"

The count raised eyes that boiled like black oil. "He is still breathing," he said between clenched teeth. "A man who would try to sully the name of my daughter with his grubby English ways does not deserve to be still breathing. He is not at home now. In Italy we know how to look after our own!"

"Papa!" Isotta's voice was low and urgent.

Miss Trew gasped, and all eyes swivelled upwards. Isotta was now standing precariously on the parapet of the loggia, one arm wrapped loosely around a pillar.

The count froze as if turned to stone. Sophie witnessed an expression of such bleak torment twist his features that she half-raised one hand towards him in a futile gesture of support. She had thought he was bereft of all feeling, but now she sensed the deep well of anguish he carried within himself, the lid of which had been blown clean off by his daughter's reckless action.

"Isotta, cara mia," he gasped, his unsteady hand reaching up towards her. "You are so like your beautiful mother! Please, get down, does this imbecile Inglese mean so much to you?"

The sadness Sophie had sensed in the young lady

now overflowed and great tears rolled over the smooth skin of her face unchecked.

"He is nothing to me," she cried, "as I am nothing to you! As my mother was nothing to you! I may as well follow her example and throw myself from here to the hard ground below which will be as unyielding as your will! I will lay as cold and broken as the marble statues that you love so much! Perhaps then I will fill a very small corner of your shrivelled heart!"

"Noooo!" he cried, the words torn from him as Isotta swayed forwards.

But even as they watched, horrified, two arms came from behind her and pulled her back away from danger. Squires had her safe. Turning, he relinquished her to the silver-haired servant in the faded livery, who held her sobbing body until the marchesa appeared by his side and between them they bundled her back inside the villa.

"Oh, well done, Squires!" Sophie murmured.

The count fell to his knees and dropped his head into his hands.

Sophie turned to instruct Mr Maddock to make himself scarce, but he seemed to have already seen the wisdom of this course of action for both he and Lady Bletherington's servant, were nowhere to be seen. Sophie and Miss Trew positioned themselves on either side of the count, and gently encouraged him to his feet and helped him the few steps to a bench that looked out over the gardens.

He sat staring straight ahead, but Sophie felt certain it was not the garden he saw.

"I loved her mother," he finally said, his voice

hoarse and low. "She was grace. She was beauty. She was life."

"Count Maldolo, you do not need to explain..."

"I do. There have been too many secrets," he insisted. "I had been conducting some business in Pisa and was late returning, Livia was waiting on the balcony. As I neared the villa she was waving and calling to me, she was with child again and could not wait to tell me her news. The doctor explained that she might have felt dizzy, whatever the cause, she leaned out too far. She fell. I loved her more than life itself and yet I killed her," he said bitterly. "If I had not appeared at that moment, she might still be alive."

"You were not to blame," Sophie said softly. "It was a tragic accident."

"I told myself that a thousand times, but it did not help; it always felt that way." He closed his eyes on the words. "Isotta was the living image of her mother, but every time I looked upon her, I felt guilt and grief burrow ever deeper within me, becoming a canker in my heart. As soon as she was old enough, I sent her away to the nuns. When I saw Isotta standing there it seemed as if history was about to repeat itself, but this time the blame would have been all mine. I have continued to push her away, even arranging her marriage to an old friend of the family who lives far away. I thought, I could then start again, perhaps even marry."

He turned his head and looked at Sophie. "I could not bring myself to replace Livia with another Italian woman. You have something of her grace and vitality, but your colouring is so different, I even considered you, but when I touched you, I felt you shrink..."

"I knew there was no genuine feeling there," she explained.

"You were right," he said harshly. "Until I allow myself to love Isotta and through her, her mother again, I am only a – a spettro - a wraith. All this," his hand gestured towards the gardens, "is as nothing."

"Papa?"

They stood and turned as one. Isotta stood a few feet away, a fragile hope shone in her huge dark eyes.

"Is it true? Can you love me?"

The count could find no words, but it mattered not, he opened his arms wide, and she walked straight into them. As they clung tightly to each other, Miss Trew and Sophie discreetly made their way back to the coach.

The marchesa was waiting for them. Her small black eyes gleamed with joy, and she took Sophie's hand in both her own.

"Thank you, child," she smiled. "You are not the one for him, but it is sometimes easier to talk to a stranger, is it not? Now my brother will find himself again, and my Isotta will not be sent away to marry an old foolish man who should know better."

Sophie smiled at her and suddenly on impulse kissed her cheek. "I hope you will all find the happiness I am sure you deserve."

"And you, my child. Go home, for whatever it is you are searching for you will not find it in a pile of old stones or a gallery of paintings. Most people are running away from something, but you can never run away from yourself."

CHAPTER 12

The Minerva was a large merchant vessel carrying a cargo of valuable white Carrera marble back to England. Its cabins were functional rather than comfortable; they were just large enough to house two sets of opposing bunks, set one above the other, with barely room to stand between them. Sir Philip lay on the bottom of one, Harry on the other. Both had their hands folded behind their heads and their legs crossed at the ankles. They stared at the empty bunk above, each lost in his thoughts.

The vessel had left at dusk to catch the tide, and the gentle rolling of the ship indicated a fair wind.

"It is many years since we shared a room," Sir Philip said quietly.

Harry smiled. "Do you remember the summer we built the tree house by the river and camped out in it?"

Sir Philip laughed. "Yes, of course. We insisted we were going to be self-sufficient and catch and cook our own food, but after one inedible rabbit stew we decided that we were pirates and so free to raid the kitchens under cover of darkness!"

After a short silence Harry murmured, "As you would expect, the reality did not match the fantasy. I did not make a very good pirate."

Sir Philip sat up, swivelled, and planted his feet on the floor. Leaning his forearms on his thighs, he looked searchingly at his friend. Harry continued to stare at the bunk above.

"You did not make your fortune then?" he finally asked.

A small frown puckered Harry's brow. "There were fortunes to be made," he acknowledged, "especially in the West Indies, but I found there was no honour amongst thieves and that I had seen enough bloodshed to last me a lifetime."

"Ah," smiled Sir Philip. "You wished to be an honourable pirate!"

Harry let out a harsh laugh. "They named me Honest Harry! I became an honest smuggler instead and took to smuggling European goods into America. But I have been homesick of late and met an English merchant in Leghorn who suggested I might be of use to him running goods into England. I was sorely tempted, but whilst visiting Pisa, this damn fever struck!"

"Thank God it did! If I had not received your letter, you might never have discovered that you were safe to come home!"

"About my letter," Harry mumbled, still not meeting his friend's eyes.

Sir Philip stilled, not sure of what Harry was about to say or if he would want to hear it, but somehow aware in every fibre of his being that it would be important.

Finally, Harry turned his head. "You know that I lost my memory of the latter events of that day," he began.

There could be no question of which day he referred to. "I had hoped that might prove to be a blessing," Sir Philip said gently.

Harry's eyes darkened with remembered pain. "It was no blessing, for although I could not remember how I came to be where you found me, I was haunted by a feeling that I may have done something dishonourable, something cowardly!"

"Not you, my friend, you were always 'Madcap Harry', or 'Brave Harry', but never 'Cowardly Harry'!"

The viscount's lips twisted in a grimace. "I did not feel as if I had been brave," he said quietly. "For although I had forgotten much, one thing I could remember was a feeling..." he paused to lick his lips as if they were suddenly dry and Sir Philip bent to retrieve something from the worn leather saddlebag which lay under his bunk. He passed a small silver hip flask to Harry.

"Gently," he said as Harry took a large swig and began to cough. "That is no way to treat a particularly fine brandy, nor will Doctor Johnson thank me if he finds his patient drunk as a wheelbarrow!"

A brief smile flitted over the viscount's face but quickly faded. "That feeling was terror, pure unadulterated terror!"

"Harry," Sir Philip sighed softly. "Only an insensate fool would not have felt terror at some point during that day. You had more excuse than most, for I saw three horses shot beneath you and each time you quickly found another riderless mount and re-joined the fray!"

Harry nodded briefly and took a deep, slow breath. "Be that as it may, I could not rid myself of the notion that in my terror I may have fled the scene. When you told me you had found poor William's life-less corpse laying across me, the idea that perhaps he had died trying to stop me deserting would not leave me. That would make me not only a cowardly deserter but also the murderer of one of my best friends! At first, it was just a vague, nagging worry that I tried to dismiss as ridiculous, but as time went on it claimed more and more of my thoughts until I tried to drown them out with whatever drink I could lay my hands on!"

Sir Philip grimaced, retrieved his flask from Harry, and ignoring his own advice, drank deeply.

"I wish you had shared these fears with me," he said so softly, his words could hardly be heard above the creaking of the ship and the low roar of the waves beyond. "I would wager my life against the chance of events unfolding as you have described. If anybody killed William, I fear it was more likely to have been me."

In a low voice full of self-loathing he shared his encounter with Miss Bowles and William at Lady Richmond's ball. "I did not get to talk things out with him before the battle and I have wondered ever since, if perhaps, the shock of his betrayal at the hands of not only his love but also myself, may have led him to conduct himself in battle with a rash recklessness that may have gotten him killed! I had meant to keep an eye on him, but I lost him in the chaos."

Harry now sat up and faced his friend, their knees only inches apart.

"What a pair we are," Harry said with a small smile. "I have not been much of a friend to you in recent years, Philip, but I can at least put your mind at rest now. I have remembered, you see. It is why I sent for you."

"Go on," Sir Philip said softly.

"William was indeed angry," Harry confirmed. "But not with you! More than one of his friends had warned him about Miss Bowles, including me. She was an outrageous flirt, but when they hinted as much to him, he would not believe them. You gave him all the confirmation he needed!"

"I did not know," Sir Philip said, pushing an agitated hand through his dark locks. "I had been busy drilling some of our greener recruits and only returned to Brussels for the ball. God knows why Wellington always insisted his best dancers attended such events!"

"William knew you were ignorant of his relations with Miss Bowles," Harry said gently. "After we retreated from Quatre Bras, he told me as much. He was embarrassed he had been such a fool and was glad he had discovered it before any announcement had been made. Philip, he was not suicidal, he even managed to laugh about it in the end, saying how relieved his mother would be that he would not be marrying anyone whose parents were engaged in trade."

Sir Philip felt a subtle shift within himself. The burden of guilt, which had lightened a shade with

Lady Treleven's forgiveness, now eased further with the ray of hope, Harry had shone into that dark place.

"I had a fourth horse shot from under me," Harry continued after a moment. "All was confusion. I will never forget the infernal noise of Boney's drums or the explosions that stung my ears. The ground beneath my feet rumbled as if a sleeping giant had awoken as the cannon balls tore into the earth all around me. My eyes were watering with the smoke that filled the air, and I saw another horse go down, trapping one of ours beneath it. I ran half-blind towards him." Harry gulped and reached for the flask again.

"William?" Sir Philip said softly, handing it over.

Harry nodded. "Yes, it was William. He was alive but grievously injured. I managed to pull him free and began to drag him towards a stand of trees where he might hope to have some cover. I had just reached them when I felt a sharp pain in the side of my head and blood began to run into my eyes. I fell. William had blood seeping from the corner of his mouth and knew he was done for. 'I'm finished!' he said to me. 'Tell Philip, no fault!'. They were his last words, even dying he knew you would blame yourself and he did not want that. I am only sorry it has taken me so long to remember."

For a long moment, they held each other's gaze and then moved together into a brief, fierce embrace. When they broke apart, they were smiling.

"So, you are not a coward," murmured Sir Philip.

"And neither of us killed poor William," said Harry.

"We must begin again," said Sir Philip firmly. "We will do better this time."

"I'll drink to that," smiled Harry reaching for the flask.

Sir Philip whisked it out of his hands. "No, we will shake on it! The last thing I need is for you to succumb to fever again!"

A shrill scream rent the air and acting on instinct, both gentlemen leapt to their feet at the same time, effectively blocking the other in. Sir Philip pushed Harry back down. "Rest, I will see what is afoot."

It took only one stride to reach the door and as he pulled it open, a second scream directed him to a cabin, a little further along the dim corridor. Without pause, he threw it open, and a large rat ran over his boot. Kicking it viciously away, he glanced into the small cabin that mirrored his own. Two ladies were perched precariously on one top bunk, another on the opposite one. He rapidly blinked his eyes to clear his vision as the pale, horrified faces had for a moment resembled Lady Lewisham, her maid, and Miss Trew. However, their faces did not transform into those of strangers, and Sophie's lips widened into a rueful smile.

"Sir Philip, you come to our rescue yet again! I am sorry to have disturbed your rest, but although I feel I have learned enough to deal with rats of the human variety, I fear I am no match for the furry kind!"

"I am surprised you did not snip off its tail for use in one of your potions, my green-eyed witch," grinned Harry, peeping over Sir Philip's shoulder.

Sir Philip felt a heaviness in his legs as the ship pitched suddenly, he braced them just in time to catch Sophie as she toppled forward off the bunk and straight into his arms.

"What in heaven's name are you doing here?" he said, bemused as he stared down into startled eyes that had deepened to the colour of fresh moss.

"You do not deserve to cradle such a treasure," complained his friend. "Stand aside. I will show you how to treat such a lady."

Putting Sophie down, he looked over his shoulder and grinned. "Calm yourself, Casanova, for you would, without a doubt, have dropped her!"

Embarrassed, Sophie hastily told him about Lady Renfrew's condition.

"She did not want us to know of it," she assured him. "But Lady Bletherington let it slip..."

Sophie looked on astounded as Sir Philip threw back his head – causing Harry to take a hasty step backwards – and began to laugh.

"Sir?" she said uncertainly, grabbing hold of the bunk from which she had so ignominiously just tumbled, as the ship pitched again.

"Lady Lewisham," he replied. "Believe me when I say you still have a lot to learn! Do you not know, that for a moment, Lady Bletherington would have relished that she had a snippet of knowledge that no one else was aware of, but that feeling would have been swiftly superseded by the desperate desire to share it with whomever next crossed her path? I only have a vague recollection of the lady in question, but of this, I am in no doubt. You may be just as sure, that Lady Renfrew was fully aware of this fact!"

Sophie's mouth dropped open. "Are you suggesting that Lady Renfrew is not ill? That she would worry us so for no good reason?"

"I have never known my godmother to suffer a

day's illness; she has the constitution of an ox! As for whether her reason is good or not, we will find out soon enough."

Sophie had turned even paler than when he had first set eyes on her and now covered her mouth with her hand, her eyes suddenly huge in her face.

"There is no need for this distress..." he began, but Sophie cut him short with a shake of her head.

"Please, leave, now!" she said from between her fingers.

"There is no need..."

"There is every need," she gasped as the ship rolled again. "For if I am not much mistaken, I am about to be violently sick!"

The gentlemen retreated with all the alacrity she could wish for.

Harry improved day on day, until before long he was making himself a nuisance above decks, offering the captain unwanted advice on the trimming of the sails and only Sir Philip's close watch, prevented him on one occasion, from climbing aloft in a sudden violent squall to help reef them in.

Sophie did not fare so well. Doctor Johnson's cheerful proclamation that she would grow accustomed to the rolling and pitching of the ship within a few days, at first resigned her to her situation. As she experienced vertigo each time she attempted to stand, she spent the time laying patiently in her bunk, waiting for the nausea and sickness to pass. It refused to do so, however. Sherry laced with quinine did not help, and as the days passed, she fell into a deep, misery-filled lethargy. She survived mainly on a diet of tea and dry biscuits and welcomed the carefully administered doses of laudanum that Doctor Johnson eventually resorted to, to ensure at least some temporary relief from the worst of her symptoms.

It was fortunate that the wind was with them for most of the journey and so they made outstanding time, arriving at the docks in Wapping, London, in just under three weeks. However, she arrived in a much weakened state and Miss Trew, growing increasingly concerned, confided tearfully to Doctor Johnson that she was not sure how much longer her dear Sophie could have survived such an ordeal.

"It has been distressing indeed to witness her suffering," the good doctor confirmed. "Your tireless, tender ministrations have been invaluable. However, I think you will find that a few days in a bed that does not move, and a few good meals will largely restore Lady Lewisham to her usual robust health."

"It better had!" Sir Philip said grimly. "And if I do not find my darling godmother at death's door, she will have some explaining to do!"

"Oh ho!" laughed Harry. "If I weren't in such a hurry to see my dear mother, I would be tempted to come along to witness you put that esteemed lady in her place! If you manage it, you will be the first!"

As the only hardened sailor amongst them, the viscount had been the only one not to take too dismal a view of Sophie's situation. "Trust me," he had reassured his brooding friend. "As soon as she is ashore, this will all become a distant memory!"

As soon as the ship docked, Sir Philip sent Vaughen ahead to warn Lady Renfrew of their imminent arrival and Lady Lewisham's ill health, and Squires to organise a hackney cab as the Captain had refused to accept Lady Lewisham's carriage on board, claiming the ship was already heavily enough laden.

As before, Sophie did not find that the world stopped moving as soon as she stepped ashore and when she discovered her sheets warmed and a fire lit in her chamber, she immediately retired, too poorly yet to feel any relief at her change in circumstance. Doctor Johnson administered another dose of laudanum to help her sleep and promised he would call in a couple of days to see how she went on.

Sir Philip ran Lady Renfrew to ground in her library. She sat in her usual place by the fire, but she was not alone. Sir Percy Broadhurst had somehow wedged his ample figure into the opposing chair. He sported an impressive neckcloth tied in the style known as the waterfall, a smart coat of claret superfine and a satin waistcoat daintily embroidered with flowers and vines. He had curly, greying hair and a pleasing if rather florid countenance. A twinkle lurked in his warm, brown eyes. His stays creaked as he leaned forward, preparing to get up.

"Don't trouble yourself, Sir Percy," said Sir Philip, a trifle shortly. "You don't need to stand on ceremony with me. I am pleased to see you here as I take it as an indication that Lady Renfrew is on the mend."

He turned and bowed in her direction as he spoke, sending her a keen glance as he did so. Expecting to see she was in her usual robust good health, he was shocked to see that her countenance did indeed show the ravages of a recent illness. Her complexion was much paler than usual, and there was a lacklustre air about her. Her sharp, silver eyes remained undimmed, however – even if the wrinkles around them seemed carved a little deeper than before – and they returned and held his close scrutiny.

"It is good to see you, my boy," said Sir Percy, struggling to his feet, after all. "It will do Lavinia good to have some young people around her. I won't pretend that she hasn't been a trifle down pin of late, never seen her so fagged to tell the truth! Had me worried for a while but as you say, she is on the mend now."

"Do stop prattling on like an old windbag, Percy!" Lady Renfrew snapped. "Anyone would think I had been at death's door!"

"Lady Bletherington certainly had that impression," Sir Philip murmured.

"Hrmpf!" she snorted. "She would turn a touch of influenza into a huge drama!"

"Was that not your intention, ma'am?" Sir Philip asked rather sharply.

"Now, just a minute you young jackanapes," Sir Percy protested. "I don't know what Lady Bletherington has to say to anything but there is no need for you to talk to Lavinia in that tone!"

"Oh, go home, Percy, do! The day I need you or anyone else to fight my battles, I'll lay back and cock up my toes there and then!"

Her words bounced off him harmlessly, and he chortled deep in his chest. "That's the ticket," he smiled. "Well, I'll be off then, leave you two to catch up."

Sir Philip opened the door for him and found himself the recipient of a sly wink. "Go easy on her, my lad," he said softly. "She's not quite up to full sail yet!"

Taking the vacated seat, he said a little more gently. "I am sorry that you have been ill, Aunt Lavinia, but you are not alone. Lady Bletherington did indeed give Lady Lewisham the impression that you were in a desperate way and it has caused her to suffer almost three weeks of unremitting sea-sickness!"

That formidable lady coloured slightly at his words. "I did not expect that you would both jump on the first ship home," she said with a touch of humility.

"Then why write to Lady Bletherington? Come to think of it, why on earth would you recommend her as a suitable acquaintance for Lady Lewisham?"

"Oh, climb down off your high-horse," she said, recovering her momentary lapse of composure. "How else was I to get news of you both? If there were any gossip to be had, she would be the possessor of it!"

Despite his best intentions, Sir Philip's lips twitched with amusement. "You are an incorrigible, shameless..."

"That is enough, Philip," she said warningly.

Sir Philip reached into his pocket and withdrew Sophie's slightly crumpled letter. "Lady Lewisham asked me to give you this before she decided to come home," he said thoughtfully, holding it by one corner so it dangled invitingly in the space between them. "I had until this moment forgotten that I still possessed it. But as she is now here herself, perhaps it would be better to return it to her."

Moving surprisingly swiftly, Lady Renfrew plucked it from his grasp.

"There, you have successfully carried out your commission. Now, tell me about Harry. Have you got him safely home?"

CHAPTER 13

A few days' rest did indeed restore Sophie's spirits and appetite although she still looked rather frail. She and Miss Trew were sitting in Lady Renfrew's comfortable morning room whilst that good lady took her customary afternoon nap, the sun pouring in through the windows when they received a morning call.

Sophie laid aside the journal she had been idly doodling in and stood to greet her visitor. Lady Hayward tripped into the room, her golden curls gleaming beneath a dashing bonnet of primrose satin, ornamented with a bunch of Provence roses.

"Lady Hayward," she smiled.

Her visitor came forward, both hands outstretched. "Please, call me Belle when we are private, for didn't I tell you we were destined to be great friends?"

Miss Trew dropped a brief curtsey and received a friendly nod in return.

"It is a pleasure to make your acquaintance, Miss

Trew," smiled Lady Hayward, "for I have heard some very good things about you!"

Miss Trew coloured slightly and bent to retrieve her sewing. "It is very kind of you to say so," she murmured. "I will leave you to be private."

Lady Hayward pulled Sophie down onto the sofa and looked her over carefully, noticing the slight violet shadows under her eyes. "You poor thing," she said softly. "I heard how very ill you have been, and I see it is quite true."

Sophie laughed. "I look positively haggard, don't I?"

Lady Hayward gave a tinkle of laughter and shook her head. "That was clumsy of me," she said. "I have never quite broken the habit of saying aloud whatever pops into my head. And it is not true, my dear, not at all, just a trifle below par. It is a beautiful day, please say you will come for a drive around the park with me. I am convinced it will do you the world of good."

Sophie smiled – her glance had strayed to the sunlit windows on more than one occasion this afternoon. "It would be just the thing! A breath of fresh air would be most welcome. I will have to change, but it will be the matter of a moment," she declared, determined that for once Burrows would get her ready in less than twenty minutes.

Left alone, Lady Hayward began to fidget. She soon stood and started wandering aimlessly around the room. Eventually, her eyes alighted on the discarded journal. She looked at it and then away again, but as the minutes ticked by her eyes were repeatedly drawn to it. She knew she should not, but finally, the temptation became too strong. Suddenly she snatched it up and carried on her progress around the room as she began idly flicking through the pages. It was not quite what she had expected: instead of the usual diary-type entries, she found a cleverly executed series of cartoons wittily drawn with snippets of speech or comments below. Seating herself again on the sofa, she perused them intently. She smiled as she saw a person who looked like a groom, dripping with water, an exasperated lady standing over him, hands on hips, a bucket discarded at her feet. The comment, *'Wherein Squires meets his nemesis!'* was written in a neat hand beneath.

She had heard of Miss Trew's encounter with the customs officer only the evening before when Sir Philip had come to dine and entertained them with a few choice snippets of their adventure. The spectacle of him kneeling before the modest Miss Trew, her hand clasped in his, great tears spurting from his small eyes in all directions – her face aflame and alarmed – brought forth a chuckle. The comment read: 'Miss Agnes Trew reveals her backbone and redeems a lost soul!'

She laughed aloud at the representations of Mr Maddock. The sketches presented him as a distant Byronic figure, but the deft strokes of her pencil had somehow rendered him ridiculous, capturing his foolishness and a certain vacuity in his expression. Various snippets of hackneyed poetry were also scattered around his image. However, the sketch where he lay on the ground, his eyes popping out of his face in terror, a menacing figure who was the epitome of every gothic villain ever written looming over him with a whip, made her curious. What had happened here? The brief comment, *'Where the Pretender experiences a rude awakening!'*, shed little light on the situation.

Flicking back a few pages to see if she could glean some more of this story, she stumbled upon a page that made her take a slow, deep, inhalation of breath. Two figures bent low over a field of wild daisies, their hands just touching, their faces only inches apart, their gazes locked. Lady Hayward felt a blush creep over her face, for the first time feeling the enormity of her intrusion; the intimacy of the scene was palpable and there could be no doubt as to the identity of the man for Sophie had also drawn his face in the sky above. The likeness she had captured of Sir Philip was remarkable, but it was not the Sir Philip, Lady Hayward knew. The eyes were gentle, yet intent, capturing a yearning and desire that made her heart skip a beat. Every line had been drawn with care, almost reverence, revealing much about the sketcher's feelings.

Lady Hayward shut the book firmly, feeling slightly ashamed and returned it to its original position on the small table by the sofa only moments before Sophie entered.

She was immaculately dressed in a half-dress of white poplin finished with a single flounce of deep blonde lace. Her pelisse was slightly shorter than her dress, of a pale blue Levantine and on her head was a simple straw bonnet, lined and trimmed with a similar blue silk and decorated with matching ribbons.

"I am so sorry to have kept you waiting," she said, rolling her eyes. "But my maid, Burrows, is a high-stickler when it comes to my appearance."

Lady Hayward smiled. "I can see that, you look delightful."

At that moment, a slightly rumpled Lady Renfrew strolled into the room, her turban slightly askew.

"Ha! Belle! I thought we would see you before too long! Taking Sophie out for an airing, are you? Well good, good, it will do her no harm, but don't keep her out too long, she has barely risen from her bed, you know. And don't wear her out with your constant tittle-tattle!"

Belle dimpled, not at all offended. "Of course not, Lady Renfrew, we are just going for a quick turn about the park."

"Hrmpf! There will be nothing quick about it. Between all the mincing fops, ridiculous dandies, and would-be corinthians, keen to show what tremendous whips they are, all the while keeping an eye out for the ladies, you will be lucky to maintain more than a snail's pace! Spare me a few minutes when you return, will you, Belle?"

Not waiting for an answer, she turned about and walked back out of the room.

Sophie and Belle exchanged a laughing look. "She is an original," said Belle, "but I wouldn't have her any other way!"

"I may be an original, but I am not deaf!" came a deep, booming voice from the hall.

Sophie and Belle clasped their hands to their mouths to stifle their giggles.

Lady Renfrew's words proved to be no less than the truth. The park was crammed full of a wide array of gigs, phaetons, barouches, and curricles – scores of riders weaved their way amongst them showing off their mounts and hailing acquaintances – and the walkways were packed with afternoon strollers. Sophie, having never experienced Hyde Park at the fashionable hour, felt a little conscious as Belle seemed to know everyone and so every few yards, she was returning nods and bows or stopping to have a brief word with a group of ladies who were ambling along the path that ran beside the carriageway.

"Belle," Sophie said, her voice hushed, "who is that man over there?" She nodded at a group strolling just ahead. "I have never seen such an extraordinary outfit!"

Belle could not doubt who she meant, for one amongst the group wore a pair of hugely voluminous trousers with wide blue and white stripes, they were cinched in at the ankle and waist, exaggerating the effect. He wore a matching waistcoat, and his shirt-points rose halfway up his face.

"Oh, it is John!" she exclaimed. "He is a friend of my brother's and a dear, although in recent years has become increasingly eccentric in his dress. If he weren't as rich as Golden Ball, his poor valet would have left him years ago!"

She signalled for the barouche to stop as they pulled alongside the walkers. The gentleman concerned kept looking straight ahead, however, and did not immediately perceive them. Sophie suspected that the height of his shirt points probably rendered the simple act of turning his head a little awkward. Not put out at all, Belle simply called out his name.

Sophie's suspicions were confirmed when he swivelled his whole body around to see who was trying to attract his attention. He had a pleasing countenance, dominated by a pair of slightly startled wide-blue eyes. As he saw Belle, his expression relaxed and he smiled, sweeping off his beaver hat and offering them a bow, revealing gleaming golden locks that were perfectly coiffed in the style known as the Brutus.

"B-Belle," he said, coming up to their carriage. "A-Always a d-delight to s-see you!"

She laughed down at him. "What a plumper! I can recall more than one occasion when you have wished me elsewhere!"

"N-nonsense," he protested, refusing to admit to such an ungentlemanly inclination. "Y-you m-must have been m-mistaken."

Deciding this was not the time to draw several examples for him, she let it pass.

"Lady Lewisham, please let me introduce, Lord Preeve. Lady Lewisham is at present staying with Lady Renfrew," she informed him.

"P-pleased to m-meet y-you," he said. "S-Staying w-with Lady R-Renfrew, are you?" His eyes became more protuberant as they always did when he was alarmed, and even though he was famed for his good manners he could not prevent himself from saying, "R-Rather y-you than m-me! I h-hope you h-have nerves of s-steel, Lady Lewisham, f-for y-you will n-need them." On that note, he bowed and re-joined his friends.

Sophie raised one neat brow at her friend.

"Poor, John," said Belle, a gleam of mischief in her quicksilver eyes. "Although the rest of us have got used to his love of the Petersham trousers and his garish waistcoats, Lady Renfrew has not and never fails to tell him so!"

Sophie laughed. She could just imagine it!

Even in such a throng, she found her eyes drawn

towards a distant figure on horseback. Although his features were not yet clear and the horse was not Alcides, she had no doubt as to his identity: the set of his broad shoulders, his erect carriage, and the accomplished way he guided his horse, were achingly familiar to her. As he drew closer, she saw that he was not alone, Viscount Treleven was also enjoying an airing, it seemed.

As soon as he spotted them, the viscount broke into a trot, only his excellent horsemanship making it possible without causing mayhem.

"Ladies," he grinned as he came up beside them, bowing deeply from the waist and waving his hat in an extravagant manner. "As glorious as this day is, it is dimmed by your combined beauty!"

"I thought you had an aversion to trite poetry, Lord Treleven?" said Sophie saucily.

"Lady Lewisham, I am glad to see you somewhat restored," said Sir Philip, coming up at a more sedate pace.

Harry clapped a hand to his forehead. "Somewhat restored? Even my poor effort at a poetic greeting was better than that, would you not agree, Lady Lewisham?"

Her eyes met Sir Philip's as she answered Lord Treleven's quip. "No, I would not," she said with a small smile, 'for Sir Philip's greeting was by far the more accurate."

Belle had watched this exchange with interest and was slightly disappointed to feel the slight air of restraint between the pair.

"You are not riding Alcides today," observed Sophie, a trifle stiltedly.

"As you see," replied Sir Phillip, stroking the neck of the rather fine gray beneath him. "He is not particularly fond of crowds, and I felt he needed a rest, even as Harry and you do!"

"He is like an old mother hen," complained Lord Treleven. "Always clucking about taking things slowly! I am feeling quite the thing, now, I assure you."

"If you insist on gadding about town at a rate of knots, I think you will find that soon changes!" Sir Philip said dryly.

It was true that Lord Treleven's spirits were up, but on closer inspection, Sophie could see he was still quite pale and thin. However, neither of them were children to be scolded by Sir Philip.

"I hardly think that a short ride in this comfortable carriage is going to stretch my reserves too far," said Sophie bristling. She knew she was not yet looking her best, but he did not have to labour the point!

"It is but a few days since you could hardly put one foot in front of the other!" Sir Philip reminded her.

"Well, never mind, we were just about to return as it happens, so we will wish you gentlemen good day," said Belle, stepping neatly into the breach.

"He is quite insufferable," Sophie muttered under her breath as they drove away. "He must always think he is in the right!"

"You will find no argument from me on that score," smiled Belle. "But the most annoying thing of all is that he usually is!"

As they neared the gates of the park, a dashing high-perch phaeton, pulled by two beautifully matched bays swept through them at such a pace, they had pull smartly over to one side of the road to avoid it. It was driven by a gentleman who must have been in his late fifties, although he was still quite handsome in an old-fashioned sort of way. Lady Skeffington sat next to him, her eyes fixed firmly ahead, her chin held high.

"That is Lord Bexley," said Belle. "He is probably trying to impress as he has recently become engaged to Lady Skeffington. He had been interested in her for some time but..." she trailed off, aware that she had wandered into awkward territory.

"But she had hoped to catch another fish," Sophie finished for her.

"Indeed," said Belle briskly, "but that is all in the past. Come, tell me your impressions of Italy. I never did receive that letter you promised me."

Sophie's head had begun to ache by the time they reached Berkeley Square, and so after taking leave of her friend, she retired to her room. The butler showed Belle to the library.

"I knew you would be an age," snapped Lady Renfrew. "Sit down and cast your eyes over this." She picked up the letter that lay on the table beside her. "Sophie wrote it to me before she decided to return and I want a second opinion on it. You may be a little bit flighty, but one thing I will say for you, Belle, you are not at all stupid!"

Intrigued, Belle took if from her. After she had read it through a couple of times, she looked up thoughtfully.

"Well?" Lady Renfrew said impatiently. "What do you make of it?"

"I think," said Belle slowly, "that she has been very careful about what she does and does not say."

"My thoughts exactly!" Lady Renfrew concurred.

The picture in the journal swam back into her mind. "But she is not, I think, impartial," she added.

"Ha! And neither is Philip if I know anything at all! But what are we going to do about it? They both have a stubborn streak a mile wide! Left to their own devices, they will slip into their old habits; Sophie will be off to see some other relics, and he will carry on in his old restless way! Why he is so set against marriage is beyond me. It is true that what he remembers of his own parents' misalliance is not ideal, but I had hoped that seeing your brother so happily married to that delightful girl, might do the trick."

Belle absently stroked her still slender midriff. A sudden vision of Sir Philip at the christening of young Frederick, the latest addition to the Atherton clan swam into her mind. Her brother had chosen Philip as the godfather and his wife, Rosalind, had insisted he hold him, laughing when he had taken a step back as if reluctant to do so.

"He is not made of china and will not break," she had assured him, handing him over. "Besides, you need the practice – you will have a son of your own one day!"

Sir Philip had stood still for a long moment gazing down at the little bundle tightly wrapped in his christening blanket. His face had twisted into an odd sort of grimace, and he had said, "I am not at all sure that I will."

"She is not up to a round of parties just yet," continued Lady Renfrew, "and neither am I for that matter. Even if she were, it wouldn't answer, for you cannot depend on Philip to put in an appearance at such events! Also, she is bound to attract a host of admirers once she finds her feet and I am not inter-ested in a horde of lovelorn swains traipsing across my threshold!"

"I quite understand," said Belle, a light frown marring her otherwise smooth brow. "Philip's mother died in childbirth, did she not?"

Lady Renfrew's gaze suddenly narrowed. "What has that got to say to anything?" she said abruptly. "It was a tragedy to lose poor Arabella so soon, but it was not unusual."

"Exactly," murmured Belle. "We can all name someone, in addition to Princess Charlotte, who has died in such a way. Philip was extremely close to his mother, was he not?"

"Worshipped the ground she walked on!" confirmed Lady Renfrew. "They were peas from the same pod. Her husband took little interest in either of them and was not of a social disposition, so she lavished all her affection upon him. The poor boy was sent up to Eton only weeks after her death. But what has all this got to do with our current problem?"

"He lost a woman he worshipped to childbirth. He was forced to bottle up his feelings and go to boarding school. He has buried them, not faced them! If he marries, he risks history repeating itself, only this time with his wife, not his mother."

Lady Renfrew was stunned into silence for once. "Of course," she said eventually. "How could I have been such a fool not to have seen it?"

Belle smiled at her. "You are no fool, Lady Renfrew, but neither have you ever been a mother, it is natural that your mind might not dwell upon such things."

"That is true," she conceded. "But you have, my dear, and if I am not much mistaken, you are increasing again."

It was Belle's turn to look stunned and a little dismayed. "However did you know? I am sure I am not showing yet. Please, tell me I am not showing yet."

"No," Lady Renfrew smiled, pleased to have the upper hand again. "You are not yet showing, my vain little puss! You have sat there rubbing your stomach for the past several minutes, however, and as you do not appear to be ill, it was not hard to deduce!" "We need a plan," sighed Belle, straightening in her chair and adroitly turning the subject. "And it must be subtle for they are neither of them slow-tops, Philip will certainly not tolerate any kind of interference."

"Don't I know it!" Lady Renfrew exclaimed. "Have you any sensible ideas to offer?"

Belle's lips began to curl up at the edges. "Do you know, I might have, at that. I will sleep on it and come to see you tomorrow when they have become a little more clear."

"See that you do! The last thing we need is for him to take another mistress, that would really set the cat amongst the pigeons!"

CHAPTER 14

V ery early the next morning just after the sun had risen, casting its shimmering, slanting rays through the branches of the tree-lined avenue, a black stallion and its rider galloped flat out through the hazy dappled light as if the devil himself were after them. The few grooms who were exercising their masters' horses, cast a wary eye in their direction and kept firmly out of the way.

'He is like a mother hen always clucking.' To think that he would ever be described in such a fashion! There was, he acknowledged, a kernel of truth in the accusation. Both his charges were safely returned home and how they conducted themselves from now on was not his concern. At least it should not be. So why was he still fussing over them, kicking his heels in town? The season would be over soon, and it was high time he paid a visit to Eastleigh. He had, as usual, neglected his estate in Wiltshire for too long.

That he was attracted to Lady Lewisham, he could not deny. That she was no longer under his protection, was also true. However, she was as far from his grasp as she ever was, for she was honourable and good and true. The way she had jumped on board a ship, knowing she suffered horribly at sea, to offer whatever succour and help his godmother might require, proved it. By God! When he had heard the moans issuing from her cabin and indeed witnessed her curled into a ball, all the vitality he associated with her drained from her frail form, he had known anxiety the like of which he never wished to experience again. Only the pleasure of becoming re-acquainted with Harry or the necessity of preventing him from committing some folly had kept him sane. Thank heavens he had persuaded Doctor Johnson to accompany them home for he was sure things would have been far worse without him.

You could offer for her. The traitorous whisper floated through his mind causing him to grimace and push Alcides even harder. He had not gone many yards further when he saw a lady in a smart, close-fitting bottle-green riding habit on a bay mare coming in the opposite direction. He recognised her immediately. Lady Skeffington. He slowed to a trot as he approached her.

"Elizabeth," he said, pasting on a grim smile: that he had even for a moment considered placing Lady Lewisham on a similar footing left a bad taste in his mouth. "How have I known you so...well, and not known that you enjoyed such early mornings?"

Signalling for her groom to fall back, she brought her mount closer. He saw that her hazel eyes were heavy as if she had had a late or a sleepless night.

"I do not as a rule," she confirmed. "But I am aware that you do."

He quirked an eyebrow in surprise, for he had heard of her recent engagement.

"I must felicitate you on your betrothal," he said. "I must admit I had not been aware that you had a partiality for Bexley."

They turned their mounts and began to walk them back down the ride.

Sending him a sideward glance she said pointedly, "Bexley would not have been my first choice, but he is a decent enough man and can give me the security I find I need, after all."

Sir Philip reached across and placed his hand over hers. "Then I am genuinely happy for you."

She turned her own to grasp his, but he had already withdrawn it. She blinked and looked away as if momentarily overcome with emotion. Within a few seconds, however, she straightened her spine and managed a small smile.

"We did not part on good terms," she said coolly. "I may have behaved badly. I wished to apologise. I am sure you know that I did not mean all that I said. I did not wish you to think ill of me when or if, I ever came to your mind."

Sir Philip felt a twist of remorse slice through him. He had seen Elizabeth Skeffington sober, drunk, happy, angry and in the throes of ecstasy, but he had never seen her vulnerable. He had taken everything she had offered him at face value, and although he had set out the terms of their 'arrangement' at the start, it offered him little comfort now when he understood he had caused her genuine pain. The conditions had been laid down by him, for his own benefit and protection.

"I will always remember you with affection," he said gently. "And if you ever need a friend, you may call on me."

She smiled at him through suspiciously bright eyes. "Thank you, Philip."

They had reached the gates of the park and their ways parted. As she turned her horse in the opposite direction, she looked over her shoulder.

"I suspect it is a lady with a pair of fine emerald eyes and a captivating smile who had you riding hell for leather down the avenue this morning. Do not let her slip through your fingers, Philip," she said softly. "If you do not claim her, another eventually will. If she has not already discovered that her independence is a hollow prize, she will in time."

Tipping his hat to her, Sir Philip made his way home, brooding on her words.

The hot, humid weather had left Sophie feeling quite lethargic. Her room faced south, and the sunshine poured in. If she had been in the country and could have found a shady tree to sit under, she would have been tempted to go out, but in town, it seemed impossible to find a quiet corner where one could enjoy the scene in solitary peace. She opened her sash window to let in some air, but not a breath of wind stirred the stuffy atmosphere. Having finished the latest sketch in her journal − (this time Lord Preeve had been the victim, his eyes bulging in alarm, his trousers gloriously depicted with the comment, *'At least the air can circulate!'*) – and not feeling like reading, she decided to slip into the drawing room and practise on the pianoforte, which was placed unobtrusively in a dark corner. She would be horribly rusty, but that was all the more reason to practise. Who would hear her after all? Miss Trew had gone with Burrows to purchase various items they considered her in need of, and she did not think her playing would penetrate as far as the library.

When she was not being called on to display her skills to anyone who would listen, it was a pastime she had always enjoyed. Once she had haltingly made her way through a Haydn Sonata, she found her fingers moving with increasing rapidity over the keys. An old favourite of her father's came into her head – 'The Soldier's Adieu' by Charles Dibdin – and having performed it for him many times she found she could play it from memory. Once she had gone through it once, she played it again, this time singing along with the music, her voice clear and sweet. As the last note faded, she jumped, startled as a chorus of applause broke out behind her. Turning swiftly, she saw five people had entered the room.

Miss Trew, Doctor Johnson, Lady Renfrew, Lady Hayward and a lady she had not been introduced to but realised almost at once must by Lady Treleven, (for the likeness between her and her son was marked), stood beaming encouragingly at her. She felt a blush steal into her cheeks. She had never enjoyed putting herself forward and had applied herself to her lessons for her own pleasure rather than to please others.

Standing hastily, she murmured, "Thank you, but I am afraid I am really terribly out of practice!"

"Nonsense, child," said Lady Renfrew in a bluff manner which failed to completely obscure the pride she felt in her guest. "You would put most of the young ladies who have assaulted my ears over the years to shame!"

"I agree," said Lady Treleven. "Your rendition of the piece was most proficient."

After the introductions had been made Lady Treleven said, "I am fortunate to find you all present, for I cannot thank you enough for the care you have all taken of my son." Her glance rested on Sophie, Miss Trew, and Doctor Johnson in turn. She regarded the last seriously for a moment before adding, "I have been extremely impressed with all I have heard of your care of both Lord Treleven and poor Lady Lewisham. If you give me your card, I will certainly call upon you if we ever need a physician. I will also ensure that my friends and acquaintances are aware of your excellence."

Doctor Johnson bowed deeply and accepted her praise with a pleasing modesty.

"I will send for some tea," said Lady Renfrew suddenly. "I must confess I have become quite addicted to the beverage and cannot wait until after supper to refresh myself with it. I am sure it is good for your health. I have taken it every afternoon since I have been ill, and it seems to do me far more good than the glass of claret I used to take."

"I quite agree," Lady Treleven said, "but whilst we await the tea tray, do please play us something else, Lady Lewisham, for I will feel myself very privileged to listen."

Not trusting herself to play any longer from

memory, Sophie picked up the only pieces of sheet music she could see, which lay as if discarded long ago, on top of the instrument. She took a long, slow breath as she saw it was Beethoven's Sonata No. 14, 'Quasi una fantasia'. It was a wonderful piece but complex. Her husband had also enjoyed her playing and again she heard his words whisper to her; *'continue to develop your character and independence'*. She was beginning to understand that these few simple words could have a far wider interpretation than she had at first credited them with. 'Thank you, Edward,' the thought had barely formed before she plunged in.

As the minutes passed by, she forgot her audience and became lost in the piece, remembering each breve, crochet, and quaver as if they were old friends. She did not solely concentrate upon accuracy but allowed the music she created with her fingers to connect with something within herself, and so managed what few could: to bring out the emotional depth of the sonata. When the final note shimmered through the air, she did not move for a moment, feeling drained and elated at the same time.

This time the applause brought a wide smile to her mouth, as still looking down at the keyboard, she realised that giving pleasure to those around her was its own reward and that hoarding her music to herself was a selfish act.

"Bravo!"

That one, deeply spoken word caused a strange fluttering sensation in her stomach. Turning slowly, she nodded towards Sir Philip, who stood by the door as if only recently arrived. "Good Afternoon, sir."

Striding forward he bent over her hand. "That was a heartfelt performance," he said softly.

She looked at him archly. "Are you suggesting it was technically lacking?"

"No, my cactus, it was all the better for it!"

How being compared to a spiny, unattractive plant could sound like an endearment she did not know, but on Sir Philip's lips, it did. Glancing past him, she noticed that all eyes were interestedly watching their interaction and could only be pleased that at that moment the tea tray arrived. It was closely followed by Sir Percy, whose eye immediately alighted on the plates of cakes and sweet wafers laid out.

"Hello," he said casually. "Looks like I arrived in the nick of time!"

"Hrmpf," snorted Lady Renfrew. "You can wait your turn, Percy, or our guests will get nothing but crumbs!"

Undaunted, he cast an eye around the room, politely nodding at everyone but looked a little crestfallen when he saw quite how many visitors there were.

Once everyone was settled with a cup and their dainty morsel of choice, Lady Renfrew addressed Sophie. "Lady Treleven, Lady Hayward and I have been putting our heads together and have hit upon an idea we hope you will approve of, my dear," she said.

Sir Philip let out a crack of laughter, causing all three ladies to send a quelling glance in his direction. "Hold onto your resolution, Lady Lewisham! For whatever little scheme they have been plotting, approve it or not, you will be ridden rough-shod over until you give in!"

Sophie smiled sweetly at him. "It is a stratagem I

would expect you to admire, Sir Philip, for are you not an expert at using such tactics yourself?"

The ladies smiled approvingly, and Sir Percy let out a guffaw of laughter. "Well done, Lady Lewisham, that has given him his own again! Serves you right, Philip, had to remind you of your manners only the other day," he said, reaching for another wafer.

"What is this idea?" enquired Sophie.

"We are planning a bolt to the country," said Belle. "Town has become insufferably hot and as both Lady Renfrew and you are still a trifle under par, and I am in a delicate condition, we thought it would do us all good."

"Increasing again, Belle?" said Sir Philip, looking at her intently. "You don't look as if you are and there is a very healthy bloom in your cheeks."

It was her turn to smile sweetly at him. "Why thank you, Philip. I always am healthy when I am with child, but it is early days yet and Hayward thinks I should take it easy."

"Good advice," confirmed Doctor Johnson, nodding sagely. "Nice to see a young lady taking care of herself instead of sacrificing her health and potentially that of the baby by gadding about!"

Sir Philip gave Belle a knowing look. She frowned.

"Do not bring up old history," she said tetchily. "I am much wiser than I used to be. I have already told Hayward this time, have I not? And he is the biggest, dearest, fuss-pot there is!"

"And then there is Harry," said Lady Treleven before they could drift too far from the matter-in-hand.

"Harry? He is not sick again?" said Sir Philip quickly.

"Well, not as yet," Lady Treleven replied. "But despite your best efforts at encouraging him to take things slowly, he was out last night very late and looked white as a sheet, this morning!"

Sir Philip nodded briskly. "I agree that country pursuits would be of far more benefit to him, but how are you to persuade him? He seems set upon visiting all of his old haunts and friends."

"I am sure when he realises how fagged I am feeling after such a long stay in town and how much his sister, Henrietta, is suffering from her shyness and wishes to be anywhere other than at a dinner, ball, or any other squeeze, he will soon be persuaded to accompany us wherever we wish to go."

Philip knew this to be true and felt a little relieved that he hadn't been saddled with the task of persuading him. His 'mother hen' days were firmly behind him.

"The trouble will be in keeping him there," she added softly, looking at him with wide, beseeching eyes. "That is where I hope you will come in, dear Philip. If you come too, he will have someone to fish, ride, or play billiards with." She sighed a little wistfully. "It would be quite like old times."

Beginning to feel hedged in, he said, "Could not Hayward perform that office? I assume he will be of the party? I had intended to pay a visit to Eastleigh."

"He will, of course, join us but not immediately," said Belle. "He has some business to finish in town first, and he is not such a close friend, as you, after all."

Sir Philip frowned, feeling himself being drawn

further into their net despite his best intentions. "I really must show my face in Wiltshire," he said doggedly. "Perhaps I could persuade Harry to join me there?"

Lady Treleven's eyes filled suddenly with tears. "Surely you would not take him from me so soon?" she said, retrieving her handkerchief from her reticule and dabbing delicately at her eyes.

"Don't be so thoughtless, Philip," said Lady Renfrew sharply. "If Harry goes with you, so must we all!"

Lady Treleven looked much struck by this. "It would be the perfect solution! Eastleigh has been standing empty for too long! It is not good for your servants to have nothing to do, you know. A small house-party will liven the place up and you can conduct whatever business you feel is so suddenly urgent. If I take Harry home, he will not rest, for he will feel the burden of running the estate suddenly fall upon his shoulders and I do not think he is quite ready yet!"

Belle clapped her hands as if entranced by the idea. "Oh, do say yes, Philip. I cannot go home just at present because my poor little Edmund has the measles and I have been advised to stay away."

"Sound advice, ma'am," said Doctor Johnson.

"You could all come to me, I suppose," said Lady Renfrew begrudgingly. "I am feeling a little stronger every day, I don't suppose that organising my household to accommodate so many visitors will be beyond my ability or upset my servants too much. It is not what they are used to but..."

"No, no, it is not to be thought of, Lavinia!" said

Sir Percy. "Not when this young jackanapes has that barrack of a place and nothing better to do!"

"I suppose you wish to come too!" Sir Philip said, exasperated.

"By Gad! Wouldn't I just!" he exclaimed. "How very kind of you to invite me. It would be just the thing for my constitution – I have been feeling a touch out of sorts myself now I come to think of it."

"Too many sweetmeats!" Lady Renfrew said. "A few long tramps in the country will do you good, Percy!"

"That only leaves you, Doctor Johnson," Sir Philip said wryly. "Don't tell me you have a desire to retreat to the country as well?"

"Oh, but that would be ideal!" said Lady Treleven. "How clever of you to think of it, Philip. When so many of us are feeling so delicate, it would be a great comfort to know a physician was on hand and Doctor Johnson has certainly earned such a treat!"

Casting his eyes up to heaven, Sir Philip finally conceded defeat.

CHAPTER 15

Having not discussed his home with Sir Philip, Sophie had not been able to form any clear picture of what to expect of East-leigh. She had vaguely imagined somewhere that would be Palladian in style with formally landscaped gardens, reflecting some of the qualities of order and decisiveness of the man himself. The reality could not have been further from the truth. She had gleaned an inkling of her mistake when they had passed a castel-lated gothic gatehouse as they turned into the Park.

The manor was approached from the west by a long curving avenue lined with noble, ancient oaks, but the parkland had been left naturalistic in style with a scattering of mature trees dotted in small clumps without any discernible pattern or design. There was no lake, but a river snaked through it, spanned by a series of simply constructed bridges of wood or stone, enabling grazing animals or people to cross at various points. The parkland flowed all the way to the grav-elled sweep in front of the entrance of the mansion, rising steeply as it approached. A deer park stretched from the east of the building, fringed by woodland which ran behind the house, up a steep hill and descended again on the west side, parallel to the drive.

The house itself was made of an attractive soft-golden stone but was a hotchpotch of styles. The central façade of the main building had undergone considerable alteration at the end of the last century and was fairly typical, with evenly spaced symmetrical sash windows. A lower, older wing was joined rather incongruously to the house by an ancient porch and huge doorway – leading to an immense hall that was still in the style of the fifteenth century, with high narrow windows, an uneven flagged stone floor, an immense fireplace and the requisite suits of armour guarding the entrance.

On the east side, a slender round tower abutted a square one with five floors, which loomed above the main building. The whole edifice was castellated, and the overall impression was one of confusion.

Inside followed a similar pattern: the main dining and drawing room were decorated in a light, if slightly old-fashioned style, as were the principal bedchambers, whilst other rooms were covered in old wood panelling and dominated by huge stone fireplaces. The tower could be accessed from the main house at the end of a dark, narrow inner corridor. However, the only time Sophie had tried the ancient oak door, she had found it locked.

The somewhat eclectic edifice did not form a coherent whole. Sometimes a small corridor or even a staircase would be stumbled upon, which led to nowhere but a blank wall. Whilst offering every conve-

nience and comfortable furnishings, it nevertheless felt
unloved and impersonal. It did not feel lived in as
indeed it was not for large parts of the year. Sophie
thought it was a shame as once she had accustomed
herself to the odd arrangement, she discovered she
rather liked the erratic nature of the building. She felt
it only needed a few feminine touches here and there
to transform it from awkward and functional to uncon-
ventional and charming.

Although she was not aware of it, she was not
alone in this opinion. Sir Philip had arrived only a day
before his guests and Mrs Lemon, his diminutive
housekeeper, had blinked away tears at the unprece-
dented advent of a house party and said she hoped it
meant that Sir Philip meant to make an extended stay
this time, for it was about time the corridors at Eastleigh rang with laughter and chatter.

Jenkins, the rather austere butler, had remained
unruffled and impassive by the prospect of the descent
of a stream of guests, merely ensuring the two
footmen knew what was expected of them, that the
cellars were well-stocked, and the silver polished to his
satisfaction. Lady Treleven may have been correct in
her assertion that it was not good for his servants to
have little to do, but Sir Philip's long absences, whilst
lessening their workload, did not make them lax in
their duties as they all knew he could arrive, without
warning, at any time and would expect all to be in
order.

Mr Charles Carstairs, his steward, also shared the
hope if not the expectation of a long visit. He had
been born on the estate, his father having been
steward before him and it was in his blood, but he was

a modest man and knew his limitations. He was effi-
cient, capable, and fastidious in his duties and knew
the community of people who made up Eastleigh as
intimately as anyone raised as a gentleman could, but
firmly believed that only the personal interaction
between a landlord, his tenants, and servants could
create the harmonious whole which he longed to see.

Determined to make another push to bring Sir
Philip to a realisation of how much he was needed
before he disappeared again, he kept him fully occupied with estate matters for the first two days of his
guests' arrival. He was pleasantly surprised that he
proved so amenable and took such a rare interest,
happily riding about the park, visiting tenants, or
discussing mundane matters such as crop rotation or
the acquisition of a new seed drill. Used to being
fobbed off with an off-hand comment to do as he
thought best, he began to harbour hopes that his
employer and childhood friend had finally decided to
take an interest in his affairs – little realising that Sir
Philip was still a little annoyed at allowing himself to
be hijacked by the guerrilla tactics so shamelessly
deployed by his godmother, Lady Treleven, and Belle
and was punishing them just a little.

Whether they felt punished seemed unlikely
however. Harry (who had the advantage of having
several times visited Philip there as a boy), was easy-
going by nature and happily showed the younger ladies
around the park and woodlands, frequently having
them in tucks of laughter as he related some of his and
Sir Philip's more absurd childish escapades. Miss Trew
and Doctor Johnson accompanied them on these
excursions, the former to lend a touch of respectability

to the party and the latter to keep an eye on his charges. However, it was remarkable how often they found themselves adrift from the main party. Lady Renfrew and Lady Treleven made the sunny drawing room their own and settled down to less robust pursuits.

That afternoon, Sir Philip and Mr Carstairs visited a Mr Throckston, one of his oldest tenant farmers who had suffered recently with an inflammation of the lung. He had vague memories of him slipping him the odd apple or piece of cheese when he had been a child. They found him sitting at the kitchen table of his farmhouse and received a warm if unceremonious welcome.

"Well, if it's not Sir Philip himself come to call!" he said unfazed, whilst his good wife curtsied low, and a trifle flustered tried to usher him and Mr Carstairs into her good front room.

"You are just in time, for the missus has made some of her jam tartlets," Mr Throckston said, ignoring his wife's efforts and nodding towards the vacant chairs around the table.

"It's not fitting, Jeremiah!" she protested sharply.

"Nonsense, it won't be the first time he has sat around this table," the irreverent old gentleman said, winking at Sir Philip. "You used to love her jam tartlets when you were a nipperkin!"

"Well, he ain't a 'nipperkin' anymore, and if you don't show him the respect he is due there will be no more tartlets for you, you old cadger!" she said, whipping the plate from the table.

Sir Philip's wide, charming smile dawned. "Please, do not worry about me, I have sat in many places far more uncomfortable than this cosy kitchen," he said, taking a seat and raising an eyebrow at the plate of tartlets which she still held half-raised above her head, a slightly dazed expression on her homely face.

She placed them quickly back on the table. "Of course, Sir Philip," she said, curtseying again and dabbing at her eyes with her apron. "It is just that for a moment it could have been your poor, dear mother sitting there," she sniffled. "She had just that sweet smile, she used to insist on sitting there too when she came a-calling."

"Aye, he be the spit of her," concurred her husband.

"Sometimes she would bring you too and sit you on her lap." She smiled at the recollection. "Not that you ever stayed there for very long!"

"Too busy playing with the dogs or trying to sneak off to ride the cart!" Mr Throckston confirmed, shaking his head ruefully. "You were never one for staying put."

As they rode back through the park, it was as if a treasure trove of memories, locked away and largely forgotten long ago, were suddenly released.

"Do you remember the time we went fishing and thought we had caught a monster, Charles?" he said as they crossed a bridge over the river.

Mr Carstairs chuckled. "Of course! You were standing in the boat, pulling for all you were worth when suddenly your hook was released, your line went loose, and you toppled backwards into the water!"

Sir Philip grinned. "We never did find out what it was."

"It was the one that got away!" laughed Mr

Carstairs. "Ergo, it must have been the finest fish never to be caught in the county!"

When they arrived at the stables situated behind the east wing, Sir Philip saw an unfamiliar horse being walked up and down by one of the grooms. Handing his mount over to Vaughen he said, "Visitors?"

"Aye, a Lord Russell has come to pay you a visit," he said. "Seemed a nice sort of gentleman. Nothing starched up about him."

Sir Philip frowned. He never usually stayed long enough on his infrequent visits to receive callers, and his servants knew better than to gossip. One of the girls Mrs Lemon had hired from the village to help with the extra visitors must have been talking.

Turning to Mr Carstairs, he grimaced. "Those accounts you wanted me to cast an eye over will have to wait, Charles."

"Understood," the steward replied. "I will see you at dinner."

Sir Philip took a few long strides towards the back of the house, paused for a moment, and then pivoted neatly and headed towards the south-west corner of the building. Lord Russell was an old friend of his father's, and he found himself reluctant to greet him at this moment when his head was so full of unexpectedly warm memories.

He soon came to the walled kitchen gardens. Noting absently that they looked very organised and productive, he strolled past the neatly planted beds and stopped for a moment before the far wall. It was covered in long tresses of violet flowers. Closing his eyes, he took a long, slow breath, inhaling deeply the faint, sweet scent he associated with his mother. He had ordered the wisteria to be planted in this particular spot only five years before. This was the first year it had bloomed.

Gently parting some of the flowers he bent and slipped through an archway behind into a hidden garden. Here borders were filled with flowers of various heights and colours. Towards the back was a profusion of orange and crimson oriental poppies and beautiful blue delphiniums, towards the front, zinnias in various shades of yellow and pink added further to the explosion of colours. But the main feature of the garden was the roses. They had been his mother's favourites. His head gardener, Jones, had been instructed to take extra care with them and it was clear that he had been assiduous in his attentions to the beautiful plants. Ranging from white, pale pink to deep damask red, hundreds of blooms covered the bushes. Seating himself on a bench placed against the wall, Sir Philip sat and let his eyes wander slowly around this haven of peace and tranquillity. Eventually, he put his hand into his pocket and pulled out the snuffbox Lady Renfrew had given him. Its bright colours glinted in the sunlight. He turned it between his fingers for a moment before flicking it open and withdrawing his mother's miniature. Feeling slightly foolish, he nevertheless held it up between his finger and thumb, so that she could survey the garden in all its glory. Then smiling wryly, he placed it in his warm palm and looked down at her image.

"I think you would approve," he murmured before putting it gently back in its box and slipping it again into his pocket.

Lord Russell awaited him in the cosy library that occupied one of the rooms in the old wing.

"I thought it best to put him in there," explained Jenkins. "For I heard gentle snores coming from the drawing room."

Lord Russell was dressed neatly in the traditional country attire of buckskin breeches, a dark clawhammer coat, and riding boots. He still looked fit and trim as he fluidly rose to his feet and offered Sir Philip a small bow.

"It is good to see you, my boy," he smiled, "although you are a boy no longer but have grown into a fine figure of a man if you don't mind me saying so."

"Thank you, sir," Sir Philip said politely. "Please, sit."

"I cannot stay above a moment," Lord Russell said. "One of my finest mares is in foal, and I am keen to see the outcome."

"Of course," murmured Sir Philip.

It was many years since he had last seen Lord Russell and he was not quite how he remembered him: his face was softer, his tone more congenial.

"Now I hope you don't mind if I speak my mind, sir," he said. "But I was a good friend of your father's and if I don't open my budget now, who knows when I will see you again?"

Sir Philip felt himself stiffen but nodded for Lord Russell to go on.

"I never got to have a private conversation with you after his funeral, my lad, but I wanted to."

Sir Philip's raised brow was his only encouragement.

"If you think to dampen my pretensions with that

haughty look, think again. I remember having to rescue you from a tree when you not much higher than my knee! Gave your mother a horrible fright!"

A small smiled cracked Sir Philip's face. "I believe you gave me a ride home on your horse," he said, suddenly remembering.

"Aye, I did at that. Your mother asked me to, she spoilt you rotten."

"Indeed, I was very fortunate," he agreed.

"Well, that brings me to what I wanted to say to you. Your father was not an easy-tempered man, but he had your interests at heart, my boy. He allowed your mother to indulge you because he could see how happy you made her, but he was worried it would spoil your character. He sent you away a little too soon after she died, I think, but he was keen you learnt to be a man. There is nothing like boarding school to sort the chaff from the grain!"

"I made many friends, there," Sir Philip acknowledged.

"I'm glad to hear it. Now, you may not want to hear this, but you are going to. Your father was heart-broken when you joined the army. He was terrified he would lose you."

"You mean lose his heir, I think."

"I do not need you to put words into my mouth, Philip," Lord Russell snapped. "I meant exactly what I said. He was always scanning the papers for news of you or going up to town to see what he could discover of your progress."

Sir Philip looked surprised.

"Aye, that has taken the wind out of your sails. He could not have been more proud of you, as it turns out. That's all. I thought you should know and as he was never any good at expressing his feelings, I had an inkling he would never have told you." Lord Russell got to his feet. "Now, I must be off. I hope you stay around this time, Philip, you are a grown man now, and it is time to put off childish resentments and get on with what you were born to do!"

It was some time before Sir Philip left the library to get ready for dinner. He paused outside Doctor Johnson's room for a moment and then wrapped his knuckles firmly against the door.

Doctor Johnson opened it in his shirtsleeves. "Come in, come in, Sir Philip. What is it I can do for you?" he smiled, firmly closing the door behind him.

Dinner was a lively affair. A little country air and a pause from the many and varied diversions of the season had refreshed everyone. Even Henrietta, who had been causing Lady Treleven a great deal of worry, had relaxed a little and although she did not initiate any topics of conversation, she listened with interest and replied sensibly enough when directly addressed.

Lady Treleven was aware that her season had been a great trial to her, for although she possessed the Treleven good looks – her hair golden, her eyes blue – she lacked the natural confidence of her brother. Lady Treleven, being a sensible woman at heart, realised that it was primarily her own fault. After Harry's self-imposed exile she had retreated both to her estate and within herself. The loss of her only son followed closely by the death of her husband had left her bereft and lost. Whilst she had not insisted Henrietta become a hermit like herself, neither had she made the least push to encourage her to overcome her natural shyness and socialise more with the local families. It had been a shock to realise that her daughter was close to reaching her seventeenth birthday, and only the unpalatable thought that Harry might never return, causing the estate to be passed on to a distant relative, had goaded her into reluctant action – her motherly instinct to ensure that her daughter was amply provided for – overcoming her inclination to remain removed from society.

Coming to Eastleigh had been a very good decision. To her shame, she realised it had been a long time since she had given Philip the thought he deserved. He had taken the opposite course to herself: his dislike of his father and his unhappiness, driving him away from his home and making him unwilling to wear his father's mantle or fulfil his rigid expectations in any way. Her own rejection of him had been both cruel and unworthy of her and after meeting Sophie, she had been overcome by a crusading spirit to see him happily settled.

Having been wracking her brains for the past several minutes for a way to bring the two together, she suddenly smiled gently and said, "Do you ride, Lady Lewisham?"

Sophie had been quietly discussing something with Mr Carstairs but now glanced across the table at Lady Treleven.

"I do," she answered a little wistfully. "Although it seems like an age since I have enjoyed a good gallop. The present Lord Lewisham felt it unnecessary to keep another horse – eating its head off – in his stables, so I was obliged to sell it."

"The miserable skinflint!" said Harry.

"I did, of course, offer to pay for its keep but he felt it would not be fitting for me to be gadding about the estate whilst I was in mourning."

"I can almost hear him saying it," murmured Sir Philip.

"Oh, do you know him?" said Sophie surprised.

"Not well, but our paths have crossed," he said.

"He is a vulgar, bacon-brained, elbow-crooker!" snapped Lady Renfrew. "Least said about him, the better!"

"It is a shame you have not enjoyed a pursuit that you clearly enjoy for so long," said Lady Treleven, adeptly bringing the conversation back to the point. "Philip, I am sure you have something suitable in your stables?"

"I am not sure I have," he said a little ruefully. "There are some fine mounts, but I doubt any are suitable for a lady."

Lady Treleven opened her mouth to reply but Sophie was before her.

"Really?" she said, her eyes alight with challenge. "I will have you know, that when I was shut up in that carriage for hour upon hour on our way to Pisa, I often wished I could take your place and ride Alcides. What is more, I am certain it would not be a task beyond my ability!"

"Oh ho!" grinned Harry. "Now that is something I would like to see!"

"My father is horse mad," she added. "He threw me on a horse almost as soon as I could walk!"

Sir Philip gave her an enigmatic look, his frown deepening. "Nevertheless, much as I hate to disappoint either of you, it is not an event that is ever likely to occur. I allow no-one to ride Alcides."

"He has never liked people riding his horses," chirped in Belle with a mischievous twinkle. "What was the name of that horse of yours I sneaked out of the stables when I was a girl?"

"Ignis," said Sir Philip drily.

"Oh, that refers to flame or fire does it not," Sophie said, interested.

Sir Philip nodded, smiling ruefully. "Indeed, he was of a fiery nature and if Belle had ever applied herself to her studies as assiduously as you, Lady Lewisham, she might have saved herself a winding and some nasty bruises!"

"Oh, were you thrown?" said Sophie, sympathetically.

"I was," she admitted with an unrepentant grin. "But the spanking Philip doled out to me afterwards was by far the more humiliating experience!"

"Eh!" Sir Percy spluttered, quickly swallowing the rather fine claret he was as that moment sampling. "I worry about you, Philip, really I do! Spanking a girl, I would never have thought it of you!"

"If Lady Atherton was not upset by the event," said Sir Philip a trifle exasperated with his guest, "I do not think you need concern yourself. Belle must have been all of ten years, and if she had taken him out again, she might well have suffered far worse!"

"Quite right, Philip," approved Lady Renfrew. "She always did need a firm hand. I am at a loss to understand how Hayward has managed her half so well; he doesn't seem the spanking type!"

"No," said Belle, a secretive smile on her lips. "He does not need to resort to such cave-man tactics. I would never go against dear Nat."

Sir Philip raised a slightly sceptical eyebrow but merely said, "I am glad to hear it, Belle, but your example highlights exactly why Lady Lewisham should not ride, Alcides!"

"Well, let the gal choose another, then," said Lady Renfrew. "If Lady Lewisham says she can ride, I believe her."

"I'll tell you what it is, Philip," said Sir Percy helping himself to a third portion of roasted pheasant, "you are getting set in your ways. It happens to us all as we get older. But I will say this for you – you keep a damn fine table and a marvellous cellar!"

Deeming Sir Percy's remarks unworthy of comment, Sir Philip looked across at Sophie. "I usually ride early, before breakfast," he said.

"I will be ready," she assured him, her eyes gleaming with satisfaction.

"But if I decide you cannot handle your mount, we will turn back immediately with no argument," he added.

"Agreed," she said with a confident smile. "As long as I get to choose which one I ride."

A gleam of reluctant amusement crept into Sir Philip's eyes. "Apart from Alcides, you may have free rein."

"I think I will join you," said Harry grinning. "For you may find you need an independent witness in case of any dispute as to Lady Lewisham's competence."

"I wish I could join you," said Belle smiling gently, "but I am a trifle delicate in the mornings at the moment."

Sir Philip sent a look of sympathy in her direction. "Never mind, Belle, think of some other entertainment that will amuse you, and I will do my best to accommodate you."

CHAPTER 16

S ophie awoke early, leapt out of bed, and ran over to the window. The sun had just risen, and the sky was a blaze of gold. Impatient to be out in such a glorious morning, she turned swiftly, smiling widely as Burrows came in.

"Burrows, we must be quick this morning as I need time to have a good look at Sir Philip's horses!"

"Of course, ma'am," her stalwart maid said, holding up a tastefully designed if unremarkable habit of a soft, green hue. "I believe this one was always your preferred choice."

Sophie's eyes narrowed as she observed it thoughtfully for a few moments. "Have we the grey one with us?" she finally murmured.

Burrows regarded her mistress rather sternly. "You mean the one that is in the military style, more silver than grey, frogged and braided in gold, the one that I picked out for you and you have never yet worn because it is too form-fitting and of a severely masculine cut?"

Sophie's smile dimmed a little, and she looked wistful. "It would have been just the thing for this morning," she murmured, "but I quite see that it is unreasonable of me to expect you to have brought it. This one will have to do."

Burrows returned the green riding habit to the little dressing room that was attached to the chamber and re-appeared with the desired one, a small smile of satisfaction on her face.

"I brought it just in case you fancied something a bit different," she said.

Sophie, delighted, gave her a quick hug – an unusual display of affection that left the competent lady's maid a little flustered.

"Come along now, ma'am," she said brusquely, "we will have to bustle, or you will be late."

"I knew it," she said triumphantly when Sophie was ready in unusually quick time. A tall hat of silver satin with a fine gold plume that curled attractively towards her cheek finished the dashing outfit off nicely. "You look stunning!"

Turning to look in the glass, Sophie gasped in delight, turning this way and that to see it from all angles.

"It is perfect," she said, elated. "No one looking at a lady dressed like this would expect to see her on a sluggish mount!"

The feeling was quickly succeeded by a moment of self-doubt.

"You do not think it a trifle too flashy?" she said hesitantly.

"No, now get moving or you will find a horse saddled for you by the time you get to the stables!"

Sophie hurried down the dark inner corridor that led to a side-door she knew would take her almost directly to the stables. Pausing in front of the narrow, wooden door that was set into the archway of the tower, she wondered for a moment what was beyond it. If one were of a romantic turn of mind, it would be the perfect setting for a headless spectre to walk about groaning and clanking its chains. Laughing softly at such a fanciful thought, she picked up the train of her skirt and carried on swiftly.

"Morning, Lady Lewisham," said Vaughen, touching his cap as she entered his domain. Alcides was already saddled and pawed the straw with an impatient hoof, shaking his head and letting out a low snort through his flaring nostrils.

"He is magnificent," said Sophie softly.

"That he is, ma'am, but I'd give him a wide berth if I were you, he needs to run his fidgets out."

"I can see that," she replied softly. "But I have the choice of the rest!"

"So I hear," Vaughen said, shaking his head as if bemused. "I only hope you've got a fine seat, ma'am, for you will need it!"

Sophie merely smiled and walked slowly along the row of stalls, tapping her riding crop absently against the palm of her hand. There were some fine hunters to choose from, but she knew which horse she would choose the moment her eyes alighted on him.

"Oh, you are handsome," she breathed softly, her keen gaze roaming over the dapple-grey gelding who had a proud bearing and was at least sixteen hands.

"Be careful, Lady Lewisham," said Vaughen

quickly. "He is a fine choice but does not usually take to strangers."

"We will not be strangers for long," she murmured.

Letting herself quickly into his stall, she stilled as he backed away and shook his head, whinnying.

"Lady Lewisham..." Vaughen said warningly, keeping his voice low.

Ignoring him, she held her position, turning her head slightly away. "Come now," she said gently, "can you not see we are destined to be friends?"

After a few moments, the gelding tentatively approached her. Sophie turned her head towards him but kept it bowed, a small smile playing about her mouth, her hands behind her back until she felt his face only inches from her own. Then raising her head slightly, she rubbed her nose against him and held her hand open beneath his muzzle.

He accepted the carrot she had pilfered from the kitchen the night before, and then gently nudged her as she cooed sweet nothings into his ear.

"We are going to have a fine run," she murmured, gently running a hand from his beautifully arched neck to his well-muscled hindquarters. "There is nothing of the commoner about you."

"You have bewitched him already, my sorceress! I could almost wish I was a horse," came a laughing voice from behind her.

If any other man had uttered those words to her, she would have felt contemptuous, but there was something about Lord Treleven's light-hearted banter that made it impossible to take offense.

She straightened slowly and patted her mount firmly. "Whereas you are certainly a commoner, sir. If you were related to the horse," she said softly, "you would be an ass."

"Well said," a deeper voice murmured. "Ne'er did Eos speak a truer word!"

Casting a glance over her shoulder she smiled at Sir Philip, gave her new friend one last pat and left the stall.

"Saddle him up," she said to Vaughen peremptorily.

He sent a quick look in Sir Philip's direction. Sophie was pleased to see him nod his prompt acquiescence, his eyes never leaving hers.

"What have you named him?" she asked.

"Apollo," he replied. Her smile widened. "Perfect."

As they walked together out into the yard he said warningly, "Whilst it is clear that you know your way around horses, Lady Lewisham, if I am not happy in any way as to your safety, we will cut short our ride."

"Of course," she said demurely, placing her right arm on the saddle, her left hand on his shoulder, and her booted foot firmly in his cupped hands.

He tossed her up into the saddle with ease.

"Thank you," she smiled, settling her knee between the pommels, quickly arranging her skirts and taking the reins in her gloved hands. Although Apollo sidled a little, a quick touch of her crop against his side soon brought him under control. Nodding approvingly, Vaughen stepped back and ceded control to her.

Lord Treleven came up on a glossy chestnut, casting an appreciative glance at Lady Lewisham. "You have one of the finest seats I have seen in a long time, Lady Lewisham," he grinned.

"But then, unless you have seen a mermaid riding

a hippocampus, I don't suppose you have had many opportunities in recent years to witness many ladies riding at all," she said dryly.

"Stubble it, Harry," laughed Sir Philip. "You will find that Lady Lewisham is quite impervious to flattery."

They maintained a decorous trot down the avenue until satisfied that Lady Lewisham could indeed handle Apollo, Sir Philip turned off the road and into the park. Once there he allowed Alcides to lengthen his stride into a canter and then a gallop. All three horses matched each other stride for stride.

When they finally pulled up, Sophie was grinning from ear to ear.

"Flattery aside, you are a fine rider," smiled Sir Philip, turning Alcides and walking him back towards the house.

Sophie nodded, accepting her due. "Thank you, Sir Philip. Flattery also aside, I will admit that you are one of the finest horsemen I have had the privilege to ride with."

"We should not be surprised that Lady Lewisham is such a fine rider," said Lord Treleven seriously but with a warning twinkle in his eyes. "It is all that practice she has had on her broomstick!"

Sophie rolled her eyes in a distinctly unladylike manner. "If I were a witch, Lord Treleven, I would turn you into a toad!"

"No, no, you wouldn't do that surely?" he said grinning. "What would you tell my poor mother?"

"I would offer to turn you back again as long as she removed you to your estate until you had learned how to behave in the company of ladies."

"You are cruel, ma'am," he protested.

"Not at all," she said, smiling sweetly at him. "I am sure your mother will wish you to marry one of these days, but if you carry on in your current manner, you will have no hope of attaching a female with any sense or reason."

Harry's face twisted into a comical grimace at her suggestion. "Marry a female for her sense and reason? You have slipped up there, Lady Lewisham," he said, "for that is just as good an argument for me to remain unreformed!"

As they reached the stable yard, Sir Philip quickly dismounted, handed his reins to Vaughen and turned to Sophie. Leaning down to place both her hands on his broad shoulders, she allowed herself to be lifted down. The contact was brief, but it was enough to send her heart racing. Stepping quickly back she busied herself shaking out the creases in the skirt of her habit.

"I will see you at breakfast, Lady Lewisham," Sir Philip said, bowing briefly before disappearing into the stables.

Hurrying to her room, she found Burrows waiting for her and a simple gown of white muslin, embroidered delicately with green leaves at the scalloped hem – the motif repeated at the wrists of the long narrow sleeves – laid out neatly on the bed. Fortunately, both Sophie and Burrows shared a mutual dislike of the increasing use of frills and furbelows that seemed to adorn the latest fashions.

"Did you enjoy your ride, ma'am?" Burrows asked as Sophie availed herself of the warm water she had ensured was ready for her return.

"Mmm," she mumbled as she dried her face. "It was very invigorating."

"And did your habit have the desired effect?" A small smile played about her lips as she opened a drawer and selected a new pair of fine kid gloves.

"Well, Lord Treleven was impressed," Sophie said, "but as he is full of nonsense, I do not think we should set any great store by that!"

Once Sophie was gowned and seated at her dressing table, she submitted herself with unusual meekness to her unruly hair being assaulted mercilessly by the brush Burrows wielded like a weapon of warfare.

"And did Sir Philip notice your attire?" her assiduous maid mumbled around the long pin which hung from the corner of her mouth.

Sophie's eyes fell to her hands which were clasped lightly in her lap. "Well," she said softly, "he did compare me to Eos."

"Now don't you go spouting that gibberish to me," Burrows complained. "I'm an honest woman and don't hold with all that Greek nonsense!"

Sophie raised admiring eyes. "Why, Burrows, how did you know it was Greek?"

"I didn't," her maid said a little sourly. "Do not tell me that a lady of your fine intellect does not know the term 'it is all Greek to me'!"

Sophie's eyes crinkled in amusement. "Of course, I do, but how was I expected to know that you were also aware of it?"

"I have served in I don't know how many fine houses these past twenty years," she replied a little stiffly. "It is my job to keep my ears open and my lips closed. I would have to be very dim-witted not to have picked up a thing or two!"

"Of course," Sophie conceded gently. "Eos is the goddess of the dawn."

She winced, her eyes watering, as Burrows slipped the pin smoothly out of her mouth and into her burnished locks, scraping her scalp on the way. "That's all right then."

Sophie was the last guest to arrive in the breakfast parlour. She was famished. Her appetite had been increasing as each day passed, but this morning's splendid exercise had whetted it even more. Loading her plate with eggs and ham, she sat down and applied herself to it with unusual vigour.

Lady Treleven and Lady Renfrew usually kept to their rooms at this hour, partaking only of a roll and some chocolate, but this morning they had bestirred themselves enough to join the others. Only Belle was absent, finding that she could not stomach the sight of a breakfast buffet in her present condition.

"Did you enjoy your ride, Lady Lewisham?" asked Lady Treleven in a disinterested tone, taking a sip of her chocolate.

Sophie's smile was like a ray of sunshine. "How could I not?" she said. "The morning was glorious, my mount splendid, and the company congenial."

Sending a warning glance in the direction of her son, who had at that moment choked on his bacon, she said, "I am glad to hear it."

"What did you make of the park?" asked Sir Philip. "It is a far cry from Count Maldolo's estate."

Taking a sip of her hot, sweet tea, Sophie considered her answer. "Indeed it is," she said. "His gardens were perfectly proportioned, manicured, and graced by the finest statuary."

"And so superior in every way," said Sir Philip coolly.

"Not at all," she replied. "At first glance, I admit they were impressive. Yet they lacked something that I have discovered is of prime importance to me."

All eyes (apart from Sir Percy's), swivelled in her direction at this remark. Lady Renfrew was the first to crack.

"Out with it, girl, we are not mind readers! What is it that they lacked?" she snapped.

"Who is this Count Maldolo?" asked Sir Percy, bewildered.

"Not now, Percy," Lady Renfrew hissed.

By now used to their odd interactions Sophie was not put off her stride, although her brow furrowed as she searched for the words to express the feelings that had been slowly blossoming within her.

At last, she spoke. "They lacked the music and melody that only divine nature provides: the poetry that is in every wildflower, the wise benevolence of every ancient tree, the lyrical babble of a naturally flowing brook, the freedom of a wide expanse of rolling green meadow..."

"So much for sense and reason," Lord Treleven murmured.

This time it was a hard look from Sir Philip which silenced him.

"Yes, the grounds here are very pleasing," said Lady Treleven. "But I think a little landscaping in front of the house would not go amiss. Nothing much, but perhaps a few borders, a terrace and some steps leading down into the park."

"Do you agree, Lady Lewisham?" Sir Philip looked at her intently.

"Perhaps," she murmured, still a little embarrassed by her romantical flight of fancy. "But only because I feel that the house would benefit from a natural source of flowers."

"How right you are, dear Lady Lewisham," said Lady Treleven. "I have been thinking the same thing myself. The rooms here are charming if a little dowdy, some fresh flowers would freshen them up in an instant."

Sir Philip seemed to come to a sudden decision. He stood abruptly, screwing up his napkin and dropping it carelessly upon the table. All eyes now turned in his direction.

"If it is flowers that you wish for, it is flowers you shall have. Follow me!"

Recognising the tone of command and hopelessly intrigued, they all found themselves rising to their feet, even Sir Percy, although he could not resist a wistful backward glance at the table as they left the room.

Doctor Johnson and Miss Trew brought up the rear. Although they had both been treated with the utmost politeness during their visit, neither of them harboured any desire to rise above their station and so they naturally retreated to the edges of every gathering.

"Whilst I have every respect for Sir Philip," said Doctor Johnson quietly, "I cannot imagine even he can conjure a garden of flowers out of thin air."

Miss Trew was less sceptical. "I think you will find him a gentleman of infinite resourcefulness."

More than one worried look passed amongst them as he stopped in front of the kitchen garden wall. The wisteria was pretty but would not make a satisfactory flower arrangement.

Sophie, however, did not seem in the least disappointed. Stepping forward, she bent over one of the bright purple clusters.

"What a lovely fragrance," she said.

"Indeed," said Lady Treleven, "this is a good start, Philip. If you would like some advice on what else to..."

Her words died on her lips as he reached out a hand and revealed the hidden archway.

They formed an orderly line as they trailed one after the other into his secret garden and then stood in a stunned silence, for a moment overcome by the riot of colour and sweetly scented air.

Sophie walked into the centre of the garden and then turned slowly in a full circle, her wide smile dawning as she did so.

"It is glorious!" she said.

"Indeed, it is," murmured Lady Treleven, taking her arm and leading her from one beautiful rose bush to another.

Suddenly everyone was talking and moving about as if every bloom was a revelation, but Sir Philip remained by the archway, tense and unsmiling. Only Lady Renfrew remained by his side.

"The roses are beautiful, Philip," she said, her tone unusually gentle. "They were your mother's favourites."

He nodded, his features relaxing a little. "It is the garden I keep in remembrance of her."

Lady Renfrew brushed her hand against his for a moment. "I know. But you are right to share it."

"We shall see," he murmured.

CHAPTER 17

When the men joined the ladies after dinner that evening, it was plain for everybody to see that Sir Percy was limping.

"A touch of gout, Percy?" said Lady Renfrew.

"It is nothing," he said, easing himself into a chair and stretching his leg out in front of him.

Miss Trew hurried to get him a footstool.

"Keep it elevated, Sir Percy," she said. "It will encourage the swelling to go down."

"Ha!" said Lady Renfrew. "So will restricting your diet, Percy, and keeping off the port for a few days!"

Sir Percy blanched at the thought.

"Would you like me to take a look, sir?" asked Doctor Johnson. "It might be that a few leeches and a mustard poultice will help."

"Some juice of Pennywort might be the very thing," added Miss Trew.

"No, no, I tell you it is nothing," Sir Percy protested looking distinctly alarmed but lifting his foot onto the stool, clearly deciding that this was the least nefarious option.

"Well, what shall it be tonight?" he said, turning the subject. "A game of cards?"

"I thought we might play Blindman's buff," said Belle dimpling.

"I think not, Belle," smiled Sir Philip. "I thought you had outgrown such childish parlour games. We cannot risk someone stepping on Sir Percy's toes after all."

"By Gad, you're right!" Sir Percy said. "My big toe is already throbbing as if a horse had stamped upon it!"

"Hrmpf! I thought it was nothing, Percy," muttered Lady Renfrew.

"Well, let us change it to Buffy Gruffy then," Belle suggested. "That way Sir Percy can remain seated. You did say that if I hit upon something which would amuse me you would try to accommodate me."

"Come on, Philip, when did you become such a stick in the mud? I remember the time..." Lord Treleven began.

"We shall play," interrupted Sir Philip with a wary eye on his friend, fairly certain that the anecdote he had been about to relate would not be fit for the ladies' ears.

"I will play cards with you, Percy," said Lady Renfrew gruffly. "If you sit sideways to the table you can keep your foot up. You are the only one worth playing with after all."

The chairs were soon arranged in a circle.

"Who shall begin?" said Belle.

"As it was your idea, you can have the pleasure!" said Sir Philip dryly.

Once her eyes were covered, Belle was led to the centre of the circle, and the remaining guests chose a seat.

Lord Treleven clapped his hands and the game began. Belle moved tentatively forwards with small dainty steps until her knees brushed against someone.

"How old are you?" she asked.

"Older than I have ever been," came a heavily disguised muffled voice.

Belle wrinkled her brow in thought.

"What gives you a fluttery feeling in your stomach?"

"Eating caterpillars!" came the reply.

When the chuckles had died down, she asked her final question.

"What is your best feature?"

"My pretty blue eyes!" came a high-pitched reply.

Belle smiled. "Lord Treleven, I believe."

"How did you know?" he asked, laughing.

"No lady would display such vanity, and Sir Philip would never refer to himself as pretty!"

Once he stood blind-folded, the players silently changed positions. He too moved with care until he felt the brush of something solid. Sophie braced herself, ready for his nonsense.

"How much do you love me?" he asked saucily.

"Not as much as you love yourself," came her immediate reply.

A wry smile twisted Lord Treleven's lips.

"What is the first thing you do in the morning?"

"Open my eyes."

"What is to a young woman hope or ruin and to an old maid charity?"

There was a momentary pause before Sophie replied softly. "A kiss."

"Lady Lewisham, I believe," said Lord Treleven, removing the blindfold.

"How did you know?" she asked, smiling.

"Too quick and clever for your own good!" he grinned.

Sophie knew whom she had stumbled upon the moment her skirts brushed against his knee. It was only the lightest of touches yet the slight tremor that always ran through her whenever she came into contact with Sir Philip gave the game away.

"What is your favourite flower?" she asked.

"The flower of the Myrtle," came his gentle reply.

A small smile curved her lips as she remembered the meadow outside of Pisa.

"What is one of your most pleasant memories?" she probed.

"Sunrise at Lodi," he murmured, his low voice sending a thrill through her as she remembered their brief kiss. The air between them seemed suddenly thick with longing and a little alarmed she asked the first thing that popped into her head.

"Why is the tower locked?"

Even with her eyes covered, she could feel his sudden tension.

"Because someone turned the key," he finally said, his voice flat.

"Sir Philip," Sophie said, removing the blindfold and offering it to him, colouring a little as she realised her question had been unacceptably intrusive to him.

226

He took it but said, "There, Belle, you have had your wish, and now I think it is time to call a halt to this particular game."

Lady Hayward did not protest but on the contrary, stifled a yawn. "I agree," she said. "I do not know why it is, but I am suddenly very sleepy. If you do not mind, I think I shall retire."

"It is not unusual for someone in your condition," said Doctor Johnson.

Still feeling a little awkward, Sophie said that she too was tired and followed Belle out of the room.

Belle took her arm as they mounted the stairs.

"So, what happened at sunrise at Lodi?" she asked cheekily.

Sophie tried to look nonchalant. "Oh, we both went for an early walk to enjoy the morning and found ourselves on the bridge outside Lodi."

"It sounds terribly romantic," she prompted gently.

Remembering how infuriated and confused she had felt at the conclusion of that encounter, Sophie smiled and said quite truthfully, "No, not really."

Belle looked a little disappointed.

"Do you know why the tower is locked?" Sophie suddenly asked. "Sir Philip did not seem to like me asking him."

Belle's brow furrowed as she thought about it. They came to a stop in front of the large portrait that dominated the wall at the top of the stairway before the landing branched in opposing directions. It was the only family portrait they had discovered. A rather joyless looking man with a stern expression stood next to a pretty woman with anxious blue eyes and a timid smile. Her slender hand rested upon the shoulder of a little boy, who held himself rigidly upright, staring straight ahead with a challenging look and a proud air. The likeness between mother and son was remarkable, but although he could not have been above seven years at most, he seemed the more determined of the two. Both his allegiance and his protectiveness towards his mother were only revealed to the astute observer: although the arm nearest to her was held rigidly by his side, the fingers of his small hand curled almost possessively backwards around a fold of her skirts, in a gesture of discreet reassurance.

Both Sophie and Belle were astute observers; Sophie because she was used to studying the symbolism embedded in the poetry and art of classical antiquity and Belle because she had lived and breathed the air of the *ton* where nuance was all important if one was to survive unscathed.

"I don't know for sure," Belle finally said, "but have you noticed how empty of all personal touches the main rooms are?"

"Indeed," said Sophie. "But then Sir Philip lives alone, so perhaps it is not surprising."

"He did not always live alone, however," said Belle softly. "And he was very fond of his mother."

Sophie's brow puckered in thought. "Oh, you are right. There is no sign that she was ever here!"

"No, yet I cannot imagine he would destroy any of her things."

"So perhaps he keeps the things that remind him of her safe in the tower," Sophie said slowly. "Oh, I wish I had never asked, I did not wish to cause him pain!"

Belle gave her a quick kiss on the cheek. "Do not

fret, my dear," she said. "I do not think that you caused him pain, but he has been used to hiding his feelings and holding his secrets close. A brave man, especially a soldier, is taught to take physical pain in his stride, but the agitation and agony caused by a strike to the heart is not openly acknowledged or admitted and so it is buried deep inside until it is forgotten or destroys him."

Sophie drew in a deep breath of surprise. Lady Hayward might be mischievous, manipulative, and light-hearted but it was clear that she had acquired her fair share of wisdom.

Before they parted, Belle gave her an impulsive hug and whispered into her ear. "I do not think Philip has forgotten but nor is he yet destroyed. It may be that you can prevent that from happening."

Sophie had much to think on as Burrows helped her prepare for bed. She was indeed tired, but her brain refused to let her rest. Sir Philip's intentions towards her were as unclear as ever. The attraction between them was undeniable and that she felt more alive in his presence than she had ever felt, was also true. She realised she wished him to be happy; the very thought that his own personal demons might destroy him was unpalatable to her. That she might be able to alleviate them was a heady and frightening thought. That she loved him was not a startling revelation, the realisation had crept upon her gradually in many small ways; the feeling that something important to her happiness was missing when he was absent, the worry and hurt she felt if his good opinion was withdrawn, or the pure joy she had felt when they had been galloping side by side, were all testament to her true feelings.

As she tossed and turned restlessly in a fruitless attempt to find a position so comfortable she would be able to sleep, the words that had been so repugnant to her that morning at Lodi, now whispered treacherously through her unquiet mind. *'Your problem is that you see everything still in black and white...but as a widow, I think you will find* there is a whole world of greys in between!'

They no longer felt quite so unpalatable as before. She did not need or particularly wish for the approval of the *ton*. She had no need to ever marry again for money or status. In denying herself the possibility of becoming Sir Philip's mistress, was she denying them both something they both wanted and perhaps even needed for no good reason? Was she really displaying her independence of thought and action by clinging to a morality that only really applied to unmarried young ladies or newlyweds who had not yet produced an heir?

You would prefer he asked you to be his wife. Sophie's eyes sprang wide open. It was true! She, who had always put sense and reason ahead of romantic notions, now found herself the victim of unrequited love! Unlike Saphho however, she would not find relief from her unfulfilled desire by throwing herself from a great height. The real decision for her then, was whether it would be better to take action and become Sir Philip's mistress and risk her heart breaking into a thousand little pieces later, or put aside both Sir Philip and her desires and direct her energy into trying to establish first, Alcasta, and then her other sisters.

Eventually, Sophie gave up trying to sleep and rose, dressing as best she could and carelessly pinning up her hair. Throwing a cloak over her shoulders, she crept out onto the landing. A brisk walk might alleviate the worst of her agitation. Relieved to find the house in darkness, she moved like a shadow down the stairs, grateful for the moonlight that shone through some of the high, small windows of the hall. As her slippered feet touched the cold flagged floor, she stilled cocking her head to one side and listening intently.

She could hear the faint strains of a pianoforte playing somewhere in the distance. Following the melody, she found herself outside the door to the tower. It was ajar. She realised she was listening to the same Beethoven Sonata she had played at Lady Renfrew's house, yet her rendition now felt like a pale imitation. The sonorous music spoke of loss and sorrow, the notes entwining in the air to create a soulful yearning that tore at her heartstrings. She moved without conscious volition up the curved stairway until she stood in the open doorway of the room on the first floor, her eyes drawn to the figure who sat at the instrument. Sir Philip's eyes were closed, his expression pained as his fingers moved increasingly rapidly over the keys until they flew through the final movement. The music gradually soared until it achieved a tempestuous tempo that rang with a passionate ferocity that left her breathless.

As the final notes died away, silent tears coursed down her face unchecked. Stifling a sob, she turned and raced with reckless speed down the dark stairwell and out through the side door.

"Sophie!"

The urgent call of her name only sent her running again, this time around the side of the house and down towards the river, the music still ringing in her ears. His playing had magnified the longing, indecision, and turmoil that lay within her. But all that yearning and sorrow had not been for her; he had been playing for his mother. She could not bear it. She must have been mad to even consider for a moment the idea of becoming his mistress! To know the depth of feeling he was capable of but never capture it for herself would be an agony beyond compare.

She came to a halt on a small wooden bridge, her chest heaving, gasping for some much-needed air.

Curling both hands around the wooden rail, she focussed on the moonlight reflected on the water and strove to regain a small measure of composure.

Before many moments had passed, she felt the wooden floor give as a steady, firm stride sounded against its boards before two large hands appeared on the rail beside her own.

"It is a beautiful spot, is it not?"

Sophie nodded, not trusting herself yet to speak. Her heart still hammered in her chest, but no longer from lack of breath.

They both watched the shimmering flecks of moonlight dance across the water like silver sprites as it flowed gently towards them, softly murmuring sweet nothings to the night.

"I have loved and hated this place in equal measure," Sir Philip said quietly. "My mother made it a magical place, she touched the lives of everyone she came into contact with. She had a gentle spirit and a kind heart. After she had gone, it was nothing to me. I despised my father for not making her happy and went against all he stood for. I joined the army against his wishes, I refused to settle down and show an interest in my inheritance both before and after his death. I made the foolish mistake of burying many happy memories and dwelling only on those that had caused me pain. In all likelihood he is not the ogre I have made him, but just another gentleman who was led by duty and did not know how to make a young, shy bride with whom he had nothing in common, happy."

Sophie's heart swelled with compassion for him, she yearned to cover the hand so close to hers with her own, but her fears and uncertainty prevented her. Out of the corner of her eye, she saw Sir Philip suddenly straighten and reach into his pocket. He withdrew a pebble and held it deliberately over the water for a moment before letting it fall.

"We have stood on another bridge far away, Lady Lewisham, and watched the ripples of a small stone spread out across the water."

"Yes," she replied in a small, wistful voice. "But they were world-changing ripples."

"Indeed, they were," Sir Philip murmured. "For my world changed on that day."

A small, sliver of hope lightened Sophie's heart as she straightened and turned cautiously towards him. "How so?" she said warily.

"It was the day I first knew how much I wanted you," he said quietly.

"Please," Sophie whispered, feeling pain knife through her. "Do not offer me a carte blanche, for I do not think I could bear it."

"Shhh," he said, placing his warm finger gently against her lips. "I have not finished."

She stood rooted to the spot as he pulled out the pins she had thrust haphazardly into her hair, watching it fall in a wild wavy mass almost to her waist, a predatorial gleam in his eyes. "Eos," he murmured, pulling her against him and dropping his head on top of her own. Her nostrils flared and filled with his musky masculine scent. She drew a long, deep breath, drawing his essence deep within herself.

"It changed my world because it planted a seed of desire and need that has steadily and stealthily grown until it has twined its shoots around my heart, body, and mind."

Taking her face in his hands, he gently tilted it up and looked deeply into her eyes with such tenderness she felt the world tilt. Her lips parted in a soft gasp.

Sir Philip's intense gaze dropped to them for a moment before he lowered his own, inch by slow inch until they met hers in a soft, achingly sweet caress.

"I want you, Sophie," he said in a low voice that throbbed with longing, moving his lips along her jawline.

She shivered as he found the sensitive spot beneath her ear.

"But not as my mistress, as my wife."

His hands moved back into her hair, and he pulled her fiercely to him capturing her mouth in a deep passionate kiss. His tongue moved against hers with the same urgency and dexterity that his fingers had displayed as they had moved across the keys, this time creating a silent symphony of desire that existed only within and between the two of them.

Sophie was lost. Sensation, perception, and emotion overwhelmed her with their combined power. Her lips felt swollen and bruised, she felt...happy was not an adequate term – she felt fiercely joyous – as though in embracing the flood of feelings that consumed her rather than running from them, she acknowledged and accepted something true and essential within herself. Her burgeoning desire was now an elemental force that spiralled like a whirlwind of flame, tearing through her, scouring her soul of any doubt or deceit until only the truth remained.

"I want you, I need you, I love you," she gasped, sagging against him.

Sir Philip lifted her into his arms and strode back to the tower, carrying her up to his private sanctuary. Seating himself in a deep, comfortable chair set before the fire, he held her close, gently stroking her silken locks until her trembling subsided.

Slowly she came to herself, for the first time taking in the details of the room. His mother's room. A huge portrait of her was mounted above the fireplace, her expression was gentle, her azure eyes soft with love.

Colourful rugs covered the floor, rose-patterned cushions brightened the chairs, and various watercolours graced the walls. They were well-executed depictions of various pastoral scenes but nothing above the ordinary. One painting outshone all the others, however. She had painted her young son, her love shining through in every brushstroke. She had captured each wave and curl of his blue-black locks, his eyes were serious but with a lurking twinkle, his smile sweetly affectionate, his small hand curled around a toy horse.

"Why did you run?" he asked quietly.

Sophie's gaze was drawn back to the portrait above the fire. "I thought you played for your mother," she murmured.

"I usually do, it was her favourite sonata, but tonight I played for you." He smiled wryly. "I was not at all sure of your feelings for me, my cactus."

"And now?"

"Now, I will never let you go, even if I have to lock you in this room!" he growled.

Sophie grinned and eased her head back on his broad shoulder so she could look up into his face.

"Do you think she would approve?" she asked gently.

"Without a doubt," he smiled, dropping a light kiss on her nose.

"I shall have to write to my parents," she said, squirming a little uncomfortably in his lap.

"Sophie," he said warningly, "please sit still or I will not be answerable for my actions!"

She looked surprised and then coloured deliciously.

"You are still an innocent," he said softly.

Sophie nodded shyly. "Edward lost his gamble. He was too old and ill as it turned out."

A slow smile of satisfaction spread across Sir Philip's face. "I suspected as much. However, he did not lose; his last years were filled with companionship and a desire to nurture another."

"Anyway," Sophie gulped, getting to her feet and walking to the other side of the fireplace. "The thing is..." she paused as if unable to find the right words. Both Contessina Isotta and Sir Philip had lost their mothers at an early age causing them both grief and pain – whilst she might never feel any great affinity with her own mother – she was beginning to comprehend how lucky she had been to grow up in a lively, noisy family. How did she explain her mother and father without denigrating them?

"The thing is," Sir Philip smiled. "You are worried that your father will try to wheedle some settlement that he is not entitled to out of me and that your mother will try to foist your sister onto us as soon as we are wed."

Sophie's eyes widened in surprise.

"Harry was right," Sir Philip murmured, getting to his feet and moving purposefully towards her. "You are a green-eyed witch."

Sophie's heart leaped, however, she put her hand out. It barely grazed his chest, but he came to an abrupt halt.

"You are the one that can read minds," she said, bemused.

"Not at all. I paid them a visit before I came home," he admitted.

"Why?" Sophie said bemused. "You do not need my father's permission after all. Or was it to see if I was worthy of you?"

Sir Philip took the hand that lay against his chest and raised it to his lips. "You are enchanting," he said. "Curious and educated but not always wise, spirited and passionate yet innocent, sometimes a woman sometimes a child."

"Then why?" she whispered, her hand curling around his.

"Because, my cactus, although I did not need his permission, I wished to show him the courtesy that he deserved. He is perhaps not always sensible, but he is your father, and wise enough to be very fond and proud of you."

Sophie smiled. "I am fond of him too. I think I was the son he never had."

"Perhaps," smiled Sir Philip. "It would at least explain how you are such an accomplished and intrepid horsewoman as well as a scholar."

Whereas a compliment on her beauty would have left her cold, the accolade bestowed on a genuine accomplishment sent a warmth flooding through veins. The wide smile that always enhanced her looks distracted Sir Philip, and he claimed her generous lips in a lingering kiss.

"Enough," he finally said, putting her from him. "I am determined to honour your innocence until we are wed, but you are testing my resolve."

Sophie smiled, for the first time understanding the primaeval power a woman had over a man.

"And what did you make of my mother?" she asked tentatively.

He smiled ruefully down at her. "She is not unlike many society mamas that I have met. Her whole world revolves around making marriages for her daughters. But she has good reason. Without a brother to protect them all, their only security lies in her finding partners who can provide for them. To wed five daughters suitably, is a hard task indeed for a family who is not wealthy and does not move in the first circles."

This time it was Sophie who stepped towards him, her head dropping in shame against his chest. "You are right, but I did not see it," she admitted. "I did not wish to thwart her but neither did I feel able to please her. I could not be other than what I was."

Sensing her vulnerability, his strong arms closed around her, gathering her close.

"How could you?" he said gently. "Your father pulled you one way, your mother another, neither accounting for those independent qualities that are uniquely your own."

At last, Sophie raised her face to his, her eyes sparkling with unshed tears and amusement.

"And did he fleece you?"

Sir Philip quirked an eyebrow. "Not at all. I am an ill pigeon for plucking. However, I did suggest that I could send poor Charles down to run an eye over his estate and perhaps offer guidance to his steward."

Sophie smiled. "And how did you feel about bringing out Alcasta? If my mother did not at least hint at it, I will own myself amazed. And in all honesty, I do feel I should make a push to do something for her."

"Of course," Sir Philip agreed. "But at a time of our choosing, and in our own way. We will take a long honeymoon, my dear, and only when we are both ready, will we engage ourselves on her behalf.

Where would you like to go? If it is within my power to grant your wish, I will."

"Nowhere." Sophie took both his hands in her own. "Eastleigh holds all your strongest memories for good or ill. We will create new ones, that reinforce the good and drive out the bad."

Sir Philip closed his eyes for a moment but then a slow, rueful smile curved his firm lips. "How they will all crow tomorrow," he said. "Our engagement will be all of their doing and none of our own."

Sophie laughed. "They will have a point," she conceded.

"God save me from managing women!" Sir Philip murmured.

"I do not think you will need his intervention," she smiled. "It is poor Harry who will have to deal with their good intentions now!"

Sir Philip's shoulders began to shake. "By God, he will lead them a merry dance!"

Sophie gave him an arch look. "If they could manage you, sir, I would not be so sure. I will own myself surprised if he is not caught by the end of the next season!"

Sir Philip pulled her close and kissed her thoroughly.

"You are a delight, my love, and may well be right, but at this moment I find I have more important matters to consider," he growled.

"Wait," she insisted breathlessly, turning her head so that his kiss landed haphazardly on her ear. "We do have more important matters to consider. What is to become of Agnes?"

For a moment he did not answer, apparently determined to search out every sensitive hollow and curve of her neck. "I think you will find that Doctor Johnson has plans for the remarkable Miss Trew."

"Of course," Sophie sighed blissfully, for a moment giving herself up to the delicious sensations that were coursing through her.

"And I have not yet heard you agree to be my wife, my cactus."

Sophie chuckled. "But then I have not yet heard you ask me!"

Sir Philip raised his head and looked steadily into her eyes, his feelings laid bare for her to see.

"Lady Lewisham, will you consent to be my wife, my love, and my companion in this life?"

"Yes," she said softly, reaching up to plant a soft kiss on his lips. "In this life and the next."

THE END

ABOUT THE AUTHOR

I love history and the Regency period in particular. I grew up on a diet of Jane Austen, Charlotte and Emily Bronte, and Georgette Heyer. Later I put my love of reading to good use and gained a 1st class honours degree in literature.

I now write traditional Regency romance novels. I like to think my characters, though flawed, are likeable, strong, and true to the period. I have thoroughly enjoyed writing my Bachelor Brides series. Writing has always been my dream and I am fortunate enough to have been able to realise that dream.

I live by the sea in Plymouth, England, with my partner, Dave. I like reading, sailing, wine, getting up early to watch the sunrise in summer, and long quiet evenings by the wood burner in our cabin on the cliffs in Cornwall in winter.

facebook.com/AuthorJennyHambly

twitter.com/hambly_jenny

Printed in Great Britain
by Amazon